—The—
Keepsake Chest

The
Keepsake Chest

BY KATHARINE WILSON PRECEK

Macmillan Publishing Company   New York
Maxwell Macmillan Canada   Toronto
Maxwell Macmillan International
New York   Oxford   Singapore   Sydney

Macmillan Publishing Company is part of the Maxwell Communication Group of Companies.

Macmillan Publishing Company
866 Third Avenue
New York, NY 10022

Maxwell Macmillan Canada, Inc.
1200 Eglinton Avenue East
Suite 200
Don Mills, Ontario M3C 3N1

First edition
Printed in the United States of America

1   3   5   7   9   10   8   6   4   2

The text of this book is set in 11 pt. Goudy Old Style.

Library of Congress Cataloging-in-Publication Data
Precek, Katharine Wilson.
The keepsake chest / by Katharine Wilson Precek. — 1st ed.
   p.   cm.
Summary: To ease the pain of having to leave her friends behind when she moves into an old Ohio farmhouse, thirteen-year-old Meg probes the historical background of an old chest she finds in the attic, not suspecting that her investigation may be linked with the old log cabin of her new friend Talley.
ISBN 0-02-775045-0
[1. Moving, Household—Fiction.   2. Ohio—Fiction.   3. Genealogy—Fiction.]   I. Title.
                    PZ7.P907Ke   1992
                    [Fic]—dc20   91-14808

For two wonderful people —
my parents

Prologue

JOSHUA RANDALL made the chest out of cherry wood. He planed the boards smooth and dovetailed the joints. He rubbed the wood with his draw knife until it was smooth as satin. On the outside he carefully carved vines and flowers, and a heart with the initials J.R. and C.P. inside it. Underneath the initials he carved the year—1774. He gave the chest to his sweetheart Callie Parker on the day that they got married.

Callie filled the chest with the linens she had hemmed. She tucked sweet-smelling lavender between the sheets. She folded the bright patchwork quilts she had made out of scraps, and the blue calico and white muslin bear-paw quilt. Last she put in the bride's quilt her mother and sisters helped her make. The stitches were tiny and even; the quilts would be warm as well as pretty, drawn up smoothly over the feather beds.

When Joshua went off for a soldier Callie kept the home fires burning. She rocked baby Sarah in her cradle and covered her up with her own blue shawl. Whenever she had an idle moment, she knitted socks for the army. She tended the garden and the chickens and milked the cow they called Brown. And when Joshua came home she folded up his blue soldier coat and put it away in the chest.

Soon Sarah had a little sister named Ellen sleeping in the cradle. Sarah toddled around the kitchen helping her mama make corn bread in the iron spider and stir the stew in the black kettle. She watched with fascination as her mother spun a fine thread on the big spinning wheel. She had her turn at the dasher when it was churning time, and by standing on a chair she was able to get her papa's long clay pipe from the mantle, and have it ready for him in the evenings.

At dusk, Callie would light a candle and put it in the window for Joshua coming in from the barn. Under the window sat the cherry wood chest, and it glowed warm and red in the soft light. Sarah would climb up on top of it and watch out the window for her father to walk across the yard from the barn. And every night when he came in, he picked her up from the cherry wood chest and gave her a big bear hug and a kiss and asked, "How's my little girl been today?"

When the last baby was grown to a big boy in long pants Callie smoothed the little dresses and put them in the chest. She helped Sarah untangle her sampler threads. She comforted Ellen when she poked her finger with a needle as she sewed her first piece of patchwork. Bread baked in the brick oven and filled the house with its wholesome smell. Soon Joshua and the older boys would come in with armloads of wood for the fire.

They all ate supper, new bread and milk, at the long, scrubbed pine table in front of the hearth. They bowed their heads in family prayer, and went to bed early, snug under Callie's warm quilts.

Joshua and Callie worked hard and lived long, happy lives. When they died, their boys, now grown men with families of their own, divided the farm. Ellen kept the rocker and the old cradle, but Sarah asked only for the cherry wood chest. Her brothers tied the chest on to the back of a Conestoga wagon, for Sarah and her husband Tom Rodgers were going west to the Ohio country.

Sarah was an old, old woman when she died and left the chest to her youngest granddaughter, Rachel. When Rachel died her relatives carried the chest up into the attic with a lot of other odds and ends. For many years they rented the farm out, but finally the house and all its contents was sold.

They had all moved west, and they never gave a thought to the cherry wood chest again.

One

MEG watched as the orange-and-white moving van drove down the narrow country road. Then she turned quickly so her mother wouldn't notice the tears that filled her eyes no matter how hard she tried to stop them.

Oh, why did they have to leave their old house and all her friends and come here to this place that looked and felt so different? Of course her parents had explained, over and over, but she could not . . . no, she would not understand. For a while it had looked as though the deal for the house in Ohio would fall through, and Meg's hopes had soared. But it had all worked out, even though the other buyer was determined to purchase the place, and here she was hundreds of miles away from her home, her real home, near the Colorado Rockies.

Mom hitched Nicholas up higher on her hip. "Come on, Meg. We've got work to do. Let's see how much we can accomplish before your dad and the boys get back from the hardware store in town."

Her mother's cheerful tone set Meg's teeth on edge.

"How could Mom even pretend to be cheerful?" she thought darkly. From the moment school ended for summer vacation their lives had been totally disrupted. The worst had been the last two weeks, with packing, supervising the movers, and finally the 1,300-mile car trip with three little brothers, an eighty-pound Labrador retriever, and a gray tabby cat who had been in the family since Meg was a baby.

Meg felt as though her heart were squeezed into a hard knot. Her parents could have avoided all this work, and the expense of buying a rickety old house that had to be repaired extensively, if her dad had only stayed at the big law firm he worked for in Denver. If they wanted to move so badly, they could've bought a house in one of the new subdivisions springing up all over Denver.

She followed her mother up the stone steps and across the wide front porch, swallowing back her tears.

"I think we'll get the beds made up first, and then I'll start to work on the boxes in the kitchen," her mother said. She tried to put her arm around her daughter, but Meg shrugged it off. "It's too hot, Mom," she complained. It was not only hot, but sticky and clammy, too.

"You're right," Mrs. Hamilton said lightly. She didn't let her daughter see she was hurt by the rebuff. For a moment she paused, as if debating whether or not to bring up a touchy subject. Finally she said, "I know it seems strange and hard for you now, Meg, but before you know it this place will feel like home. The country really is a wonderful place to live. It's different from what we were used to in Colorado, but there are many good things here, too. Soon this will seem like home to all of us." She waited for Meg to say something, but after a long moment went on up the stairs with a sigh.

Meg couldn't trust herself to speak. Anyway, she'd heard it all before a hundred times. Sulky, she followed her mother through the house and upstairs. She let her hand trail up the smooth dark walnut of the handrail. Well, her mother was right about one thing—it would certainly be different here. This old farmhouse had two stories—three, really, including the attic. She hadn't been up there yet, but Dad said the whole top floor was just one large room full of junk and cobwebs. Back home in Colorado everything was on the same level. All these stairs would be another adjustment to make.

She followed her mother into the room she had been allowed to pick out. Of course there had only been one real choice, but her parents had made a big deal out of it. Nicholas, being the baby, had to have the room closest to her parents, and Daniel, who was five, shared the room with him. Micah was an eight-year-old G.I. Joe freak, and demanded the ugly tan room at the very back of the house. ("All right! Khaki!" he yelled when he saw it. Micah almost always yelled.)

So she chose the room that had wallpaper, slightly faded, with tiny, pale pink rosebuds and stripes, and Mom smiled her approval. There were two big windows that looked out into the leafy green branches of an old tree, an apple tree, Dad said. The wooden floor was made of wide pine boards, warm brown with age. It was a nice room, Meg supposed, but it didn't seem like it was really her room. *Her* room was back in the Denver suburb of Littleton, with kids she had grown up with living right down the street. The knot grew tight again in her chest, until it hurt to breathe.

She thought of her three very best friends Alicia and Gabby and Heather, and felt tears start to well up again in her eyes. They always had such fun together in her old room, back in Littleton. For sleep-overs the four of them would bunch together into sleeping bags on the floor. It was always very crowded, but that added to the general hilarity. Usually sometime way past midnight her mother would have to come in and tell them to stop giggling and go to sleep.

Meg looked around at her new light, pretty room. It was filled with her old furniture, but empty just the same. She knew she would never feel at home here, ever. All she could feel was the knot in her chest.

Mrs. Hamilton left Nicholas with Meg and went to find the boxes marked bedding. Meg idly watched her baby brother crumble up a soggy graham cracker while she thought about this new place they had moved to. Dad said the house had once been part of a large farm, and one of the reasons they bought it was because they could purchase twenty acres of land with it. The rest of the farmland had been sold to neighboring farmers years before. There weren't many houses around, not even any sidewalks—just trees and fields as far as you could see. And it was four miles to the nearest town, called Lebanon. "If you can even call it a town," Meg thought bitterly. "It doesn't even have a mall. We'll have to drive all the way to Cincinnati or Dayton to shop."

Her father had lived all over the country as a boy growing up, but he had gone to college in Ohio, and had always wanted to move back there. "I think some distant relatives lived in Ohio at one time. In fact, they were early settlers, so the story goes in the family. Maybe that's why I feel that's where my roots are," he used to say.

When the job became available in a small law firm in the western part of the state, her parents decided it would be a great opportunity to leave what they thought was the hectic life of the Denver suburbs. They didn't think it would be hard to get used to living in the country. "The Midwest is such a friendly place," Dad told them, but more especially her, because she was the only one upset at the prospect of moving. "And Lebanon is one of the prettiest towns in Ohio. The countryside is rolling and green; it's settled land, gentle. You'll soon make plenty of new friends."

"Oh, no I won't," she thought grimly. She'd show her father and mother that they were wrong. "What about my feelings? What about the things I want?" Meg wiped gooey graham cracker clumps off the baby's face, and he grinned at her with all four of his new white teeth.

"How can you smile?" she asked him with a glowering look. "Don't you realize my whole life is ruined?"

Her mother came in, and together, silently, they spread pale green sheets and a white summer blanket on her bed.

The boy had ridden his dilapidated bike slowly past the house four times before Meg came down off the front steps. She had been loading books into the shelves in the living room—the front parlor, Mom called it—when the noise brought her to the porch. The bike had bits of faded green and silver paint on it along with lots of rust. It had fat balloon tires, and the front and back fenders looked as if they were held in place with bubble gum or masking tape. The fenders clattered and the whole bike shook as the boy pumped up and down the road. A wire basket on the front handlebars was filled with books.

Meg wanted to stay in the house and ignore the boy, but she found she couldn't. He was the only kid her age that she had seen around here. For all she knew, he might be the only kid there was in the whole state of Ohio.

Her feet took her unwillingly down the brick walk. Looking around desperately for some excuse to be near the road, she began to fiddle with the flag on the mailbox. She would pretend it needed to be tightened. She didn't want him to think she'd walked outside just to meet him.

He rode by again, and this time he stopped. She knew the boy was watching her, waiting for her to look up. She studied the mailbox flag intently.

"Hi," he finally said.

Now she allowed herself to look up. The first thing she noticed was his freckles, then a round face and funny outdated round glasses in front of round blue eyes. His bright red hair was plastered damply across his forehead. She'd never seen so many freckles.

"I guess you just moved in here." That was a brilliant observation. "I live down the road. My name's Talley. Talley Gradey."

Right then and there she decided she didn't want to talk to this dumb-looking boy with a funny name, but she figured she had to be polite. "After all," she thought hope-fully, "maybe he has a sister."

"I'm Meg Hamilton." She hardly glanced at him, but kept toying with the red flag. "We moved in yesterday. From Colorado." Great. A boy right next door. Or right down the road. "Why couldn't it have been a girl?" she asked silently. A picture of her friends back in Littleton, the girls on her block, jumped into her mind. They all walked to school together and shared one another's clothes. They wrote each other endless notes always signed "BFF"— best friends forever.

And what did she have here in Ohio? An old white

farmhouse on a boring country road and a boy with a ridiculous name and freckles.

She couldn't help but feel a little curious about him. She continued to twist the mail flag up and down while she watched him out of the corner of her eye.

Talley pushed his bike across the road and let it fall with a crash into the honeysuckle on the bank by their mailbox. Miraculously, the books all stayed in the basket. He sat down on the flagstone step, and looked at her expectantly. Oh, brother!

"What grade will you be in this year?" he asked to the back of her head. Meg slowly turned around. Suddenly she didn't want to talk to him. She didn't want to make any new friends. Maybe if she answered his questions he'd leave soon.

"Eighth," she replied shortly. She hoped this kid wouldn't become a pest. What did he say his name was, anyway—Sally Gravy or Talley Gradey? The rhyme was so silly it made her smile, and the dumb kid thought she was smiling at him, and gave her a big grin.

"I'll be in seventh. That means we'll be in the same school. Grover Cleveland Middle School." Talley pulled a blade of grass out of the honeysuckle and settled more comfortably with his back against the top step.

Meg frowned. "Great," she thought. "Not only do I have to put up with a boy next door, but he's a year younger than I am. Double great! And Grover Cleveland? It sounds like the middle school was named for a character from 'Sesame Street'!"

She thought of Anasazi Intermediate back in Littleton, named for the ancient Indian cliff dwellers of the Southwest. The school had only been built the year before, and everything was new and bright and modern. The halls were painted with designs taken from Indian pottery—birds, fish, and other animal symbols—all colored with the delicate hues of the mesas and mountains. She and her friends were planning to have lockers next to each other in Eighth Grade Alley, far away from the lowly sixth and seventh graders. The lockers for eighth graders were turquoise blue, as bright as the western sky. Here in Ohio, at Grover Cleveland, the lockers were probably olive drab. Or pale gray. She looked up at the sky. It hadn't been clear since they got here. Did the sun ever shine in Ohio?

There didn't seem to be anything more to say to this odd little boy. She certainly didn't want him to get the idea that she wanted to be friends or anything. Meg squirmed uncomfortably in the silence, but Talley didn't seem to notice. Something about this boy made her mad. His eyes were too round and intelligent, his face too angelic. He looked too happy. It made Meg angry to see someone so happy, when she was intent on being so miserable.

"What's he sticking around for, anyway," she thought crossly, "an invitation for lunch?"

Maybe he could play with Micah. She was about to ask him if he liked G.I. Joe when the back screen door slammed, and Dad came around the corner of the house with a bucket. Their black Lab, Callahan, galloped along right on his heels.

"Hey, Punkin, Mom's put us to work." He jerked his head toward the house. "All the downstairs windows before lunch. Think we can do it?" He put the bucket down and walked over with his hand out to the boy. "Hi there," he said easily. "I'm Kenneth Hamilton."

Talley was already on his feet. "Hello, sir. My name is Talley Gradey. I live just through the woods, that way." He indicated the direction of his house with his hand. He sounded much older than someone who had just barely finished the sixth grade, and his relaxed, friendly manner made Meg even more annoyed.

To make matters worse, Callahan was making a total idiot of himself, black tail furiously wagging every which way as he made friends. Talley dropped to his knees, scratching Callahan behind the ears.

"This is a great dog!" he told her father. Cal was loving every minute of it. He licked Talley's cheek.

"Traitor! See if I fix you your dinner tonight," Meg thought blackly.

Finally she couldn't stand it any longer. Her dad was talking to this Sally-Talley as though they'd known each other for years. It was too much! She threw herself away from where she was leaning against the mailbox and picked up the steaming bucket of ammonia water.

"We've got work to do, Dad," she said pointedly. "See you around, Talley." She stalked toward the house stiffly, but with contrived nonchalance, like a cat walking away from a fight.

Watching Meg walk off, Kenneth Hamilton shrugged his shoulders at Talley with a puzzled look. They grinned at each other like old friends as the boy gave a good-bye pat to Callahan and picked up his bike. Meg didn't turn her head to watch, but she heard him ride off down the road with a metallic clatter.

—Two—

THE rollicking flutes, fiddles, and Irish harps of a Chieftains tape floated through the open windows, a sure sign that Mom was cleaning house.

Meg had spent the morning keeping Nicholas and Daniel amused, and it was not much fun. Of course she loved her little brothers, and usually didn't mind tending them, but this morning she felt tired and all out of sorts. Another gray day, and hot, just like the ones before them, full of boxes to be unpacked and nothing looking right or feeling like home. The pieces of furniture Meg had grown up with looked as strange and out of place here in Ohio as she felt.

She had spread a blanket on the back porch, and Nicholas was busily stacking blocks and then knocking them down. He hit the most recently built tower with his arm and crowed with laughter as the blocks scattered off the blanket and across the floor of the porch.

Carin Hamilton came to the back door and watched as her daughter retrieved the wooden blocks and set them in front of Nicholas again. "That's about the hundredth time he's done that," Meg complained peevishly.

"That's what makes it fun," her mother answered with a smile. She came out onto the porch. "Gosh, it's warm out here. Not much of a breeze, is there?" She fanned herself with the blue-and-white striped butcher's apron she had just taken off.

Meg bit back a nasty reply to that understatement of the century. *Warm?* It was like an oven, and the sun wasn't even out. Her light T-shirt was stuck to her back and her thick, brown, shoulder-length hair felt hot and wet on her neck. It was another overcast day, like all the days so far in Ohio. Today the air was so still and heavy that it actually seemed hard to breathe.

Meg couldn't help comparing it to Colorado. No matter how warm it got back home in Littleton, there was always a bit of a breeze. The air there was dry, invigorating. In Ohio it was heavy with moisture, and it made Meg feel heavy and dull.

Mom picked the baby up and buried her face in his tummy. Nicholas squealed with laughter and clutched at her hair with his dimpled baby hands.

"Ready for lunch and a nap, little man?" she asked him. "And how about you, Daniel? Hey, what have you built there?"

Daniel proudly held up a confused mass of red, blue, and white plastic blocks. "It'th a thpace thtation," he told her. "It'th for intergalactic communicationth." He didn't even stumble over the big words. Meg thought the thing he'd built looked more like some sort of mutant octopus, but she had to smile at him even though she didn't really feel like smiling at anything. Daniel could be so serious at times that it had to make you laugh. And his lisp was adorable.

Their mother studied the Loc Blocs carefully, displaying a level of patience that Meg could never imagine reaching. "It's a wonderful space station, Daniel," she told him seriously. "Meg"—her mother turned back to her—"why don't you take a bike ride around the neighborhood until dinnertime? You've been busy helping us get settled, and I think you deserve a little time off."

Until dinnertime! That was a death sentence! Meg gave a snort that didn't quite sound like laughter. The awful achy knot was back, and it felt bigger than ever.

"That's a joke!" she told her mother. "I don't know what in the world I can do for that long around here."

Her mother calmly brushed back a few wisps of streaky blond hair from her forehead. "How about going to see that boy who stopped by here the other day? He seemed about your age, and he was certainly friendly."

Meg bristled. "How can you stand there and tell me who to be friends with? I don't have anything in common with him—with Sally Gravy—and I don't want to be his friend!"

"Okay," her mother said quietly. "You could go exploring. Find out what the countryside is like around here."

Hot anger boiled up inside of Meg. "I *know* what it's like here! Fields and farms and lots of nothing! No neighbors, no sidewalks, no stores—just nothing! I hate it here!" she cried at her mother. "I want to go back to Colorado. I never wanted to come here!" Now Meg was sobbing. "I hate it here and there's nothing that will ever change my mind! And I hate you, too!" The words were out before she realized it, hanging on the still air as if they had been written there.

Meg turned and ran blindly, choking back sobs. In her mind she could still see her mother standing there, holding Nicholas, with a pained expression on her face; and Daniel, staring up at her with huge eyes and mouth hanging open in shock.

She discovered she had reached the barn. The side door was just to her left. She pulled it open and went in. Inside was dim and still. The smell of dust, hay, and motor oil were stifling in the heat.

Meg leaned her back against the door and cried. She felt like she had held it in for days, ever since they'd arrived here. Now it felt good to let it out. "I just want to go home!" she sobbed over and over again. "I hate it here!"

After a time the tears stopped. She coughed and wiped her nose with the back of her hand and wished she had a tissue. She had no idea how long she'd been there in the barn crying, but she was exhausted, drained. Her head felt as though it weighed a hundred pounds, and she knew her eyes were swollen, her face red and blotchy.

The quiet in the barn was the first thing she became aware of. She imagined she could almost hear her heart beating.

Odds and ends of lumber were stacked against the walls. Ropes and pieces of leather—old harnesses?—hung from wooden pegs. High up, in what was the floor of the loft, wisps of hay stuck through the cracks between the boards. Large square beams ran the whole width of the big room.

She noticed the ladder to the loft. The wood was old and dry, but the ladder was solid. She reached the top and clumsily heaved herself up and into the loft. The space was not very big. Dust motes danced in the light from a window high up in the wall, and a dozen or so broken bales of hay, dusty and stale smelling, lay scattered about.

She jumped as the old building creaked and something scurried away through the hay. The noise was enormous in the ageless quiet of the barn. She shivered and clung to the post at the top of the ladder as she looked around carefully.

The mouse or whatever had made the rustling sound was gone. Looking before she stepped, Meg made her way over to the bales of hay. In spite of the great age and obvious neglect of the barn, the wide floorboards were firm.

She sat down on one of the bales of hay, leaning wearily back against another. "I'll just stay up here," she thought unreasonably, "I'll stay up here forever." But even though she tried, she couldn't summon up the terrible rage of a few moments ago. She felt numb, oddly tranquil, and very tired.

Her neck itched, and Meg sat up, groggy and suddenly itchy all over. Her eyes flew open wide and she sat up quickly as she realized she had fallen asleep. She was covered with strands of hay and dust. She brushed herself off and climbed down the ladder.

"I must be a mess," she thought. The house sat there appealingly across the lawn, and she started toward it, but stopped. She saw again the hurt and pain on her mother's face, the horror on Daniel's, and decided she couldn't face them.

A water spigot stood up out of a bed of mint along the side of the barn. She twisted the handle and water gurgled out, slow and warm at first, then faster and achingly cold. Meg splashed the water all over her face and neck and gasped with the coldness of it. She picked a sprig of the mint and rubbed it in her hands, then picked another piece and chewed it. Making a cup with her hands, she drank. The water hit her throat and cleared away the fuzziness of crying and sleep.

When she'd had enough, she turned off the spigot tight, so it wouldn't drip, and walked around the side of the barn.

Against the stone foundation grew a riot of ferns and more mint. Grasshoppers clicked noisily and flew up in front of her as she walked through the grass. "Someone must have mowed it before we moved in," she thought idly. "Dad will need a riding mower to keep it all cut." She hadn't really ever thought about how large the property was.

In Colorado they had just had a small lot, only room enough for a little grass, with houses almost exactly alike surrounding them on all sides. Now she walked around the barn and noticed a large fenced area, with grass and weeds a couple of feet high in places. On the other side of the pasture was a stream, and beyond the stream rose the tall trees of a woodland.

The thought of wading was irresistible. Meg climbed through the fence and broke into a run across the pasture to the edge of the water. The stream was lovely. It was so narrow in places that it could be jumped over, and at those places the water flowed swiftly, bubbling over mossy brown rocks. In other places the stream widened into quiet, shallow pools. There was a path on the other side of it, and without thinking, Meg jumped across and started walking.

The surface of the path was smooth and packed hard, as if the trail received a lot of use. "Who uses it?" she wondered. All the country on the other side of the stream was empty, there was just the woods as far as she could see.

The path followed the snakelike route of the stream. The ground rolled gently down, and the water jumped and splashed within its boundary of rocks. Almost at once the trees closed in. Meg was struck by the difference between this country and the place where she had grown up.

To get to any kind of forest, you had to drive up to the mountains in Colorado. Otherwise, the land was empty, with scattered pinyon trees and grasses and tumbleweeds. It was high plains country, very dry, and trees would only grow up in the mountains where there was more moisture, or in the few river valleys.

Once you drove up, away from the suburban sprawl of the Denver area, you entered another world. Gradually, as you climbed, it got greener, and the trees got thicker and taller. First pinyon mixed with cedar, then the towering ponderosa pines. Pretty soon darker green spruce would appear, and finally the stands of aspen.

In the fall, the aspens turned a clear, pure yellow. Whole mountainsides would become golden, with patches of dark green pines.

The smell of the western forest, her forest, was different, too, and so much better. The moment you started to climb up through the pines you could smell their clean, sharp scent.

The wind always was moving in those beautiful mountains—not still and quiet like these Ohio woods. Sometimes it would whip through the trees, lashing them, with a loud moaning sound. At other times it would whisper gently, moving whole mountainsides of trees softly. It was never totally silent.

Meg had walked a good distance by now, and could barely see the faded red of the back of their barn up through the trees behind her. Ahead was a clearing. She reached the edge of the woods abruptly, and there, right in front of her, was an odd little house with some run-down looking outbuildings and a woodpile against it almost as tall as the front porch roof.

It wasn't like the witch's house in Hansel and Gretel, all candy and gingerbread, although the way Meg came upon it so suddenly reminded her of that old fairy tale. This one was part rough stone and part dark brown logs striped with white chinking. The roof was made of flat blue-gray slates, and green moss was growing on it in patches. A climbing rosebush covered the posts and railings of the porch, a mass of red blooms. The whole place looked as if it had just grown right up out of the floor of the woods. It looked as if it had stood there forever. The house was very small, and Meg stood still, squinting her eyes in the brighter light of the clearing. Maybe that was why she didn't notice the person sitting on the front porch at first.

As she stood there, she noticed that it wasn't very bright anymore. In the woods she hadn't seen the black clouds building overhead. The wind started to blow, and a deafening clap of thunder, right overhead, made Meg almost jump out of her skin. She looked up, and above and behind her, over the tops of the trees, she saw blue-black rolling clouds, and suddenly felt afraid.

"Meg? Hey, Meg! Come on over, before the rain starts!" a vaguely familiar voice yelled. Large drops began to fall as she crossed the clearing. She started to run and was almost to the porch before she realized that the voice belonged to Talley Gradey.

—*Three*—

THE pale greeny-gray undersides of the leaves showed in the wind. Lightning made the clearing brighter than bright sunshine for an instant. Thunder bellowed again, and Meg was very glad she had shelter, even if it was with that dumb Talley Gradey.

Talley sat on a rocking chair with a book in his lap. There was a painting of pirates on the cover. Pointing out to the rain, which was coming down in gray sheets now, he said, "You just made it," and grinned at her. It was a funny kind of grin—it made you want to grin back, even when you tried not to.

She managed to hold back the grin and gave instead a small smile which somehow didn't feel at all good. "I didn't know you lived here. I was just following the path," she told him. She didn't want him to think she had come on purpose to see him, for goodness' sake.

"So you've been exploring the Little Peavine," Talley said.

Meg thought she didn't hear him right. "The what?"

"The creek. It's called Little Peavine Creek," he explained. "Historically speaking, it was prominent in the eighteen thirties and forties and fifties. Escaped slaves used to follow it up from Cincinnati as part of the Underground Railroad."

"Gosh," Meg said weakly. She wondered if Talley was always such a well of information. She tried to remember if she had ever learned anything about the Underground Railroad at school. History had never seemed very interesting; she seldom thought much about it.

From inside the house a quivery voice called out. "Talmadge, you'd best come in here out of the storm. That lightning is a tad too close."

Talley turned toward the open door and called back, "Right away, Mim." He looked at Meg and pushed his round glasses up on his nose. "That's my great-grandmother. Would you like to come in?" Meg hesitated. Did she really want to go inside Talley's house? "We ought to get in away from the lightning," Talley continued. "You can call your mother and tell her where you are."

Meg felt a stab of guilt at the thought of her mother. She didn't really want to talk to her, even on the phone, but she knew she had to. "Yeah, I guess I'd better do that. My mom will be worried, probably." With a glance over her shoulder at the rain, she followed Talley Gradey into the funny little house.

It was dark and gloomy inside. They walked into a section of the house made out of logs. Meg had been in log houses before. When they went skiing at Aspen once they stayed in a cabin that was shiny and new, with big logs of a light golden color.

This little log room of Talley's was nothing like the log cabin at Aspen. The ceiling was so low that Meg had to fight the urge to duck her head. What small amount of light there was came through two inadequate windows. Instead of the gorgeous, lightly finished wood logs of the ski cabin, this place had dark brown logs alternating with a white filler, just like the outside.

As her eyes grew accustomed to the dim light, Meg looked around the little room. There was not much space for furniture. In front of the wide stone fireplace was a small couch with a curved back. Against one wall stood a dresser or wardrobe that very nearly reached the low ceiling. In front of one of the windows was a small table, and next to it a pair of rocking chairs.

The woman in the rocking chair was so tiny and so still that Meg overlooked her for a moment. Talley stood by the chair and said softly, "Mim? I'd like you to meet someone." He motioned for her to come closer. "This is Meg Hamilton. They just moved into the old Rodgers place."

Meg had thought the old woman was asleep, or maybe even dead, she was so still, but the dark eyes in that horribly wrinkled and puckered face were lively and bright. Mim's eyes darted over Meg, sharp and quick, and her face wrinkled, impossibly, even more, as she smiled a wide grin that was exactly like Talley's.

"The old Rodgers place, you say? Well, well. So there will be a nice young family in there again, will there? I'm very glad of that." She reached out a small, withered hand, and Meg realized with dread that she was expected to shake it.

Meg stuck out her hand and took Mim's. What else could she do? Talley stood there with that dumb grin on his face and Mim's black eyes looked at her expectantly. The tiny hand felt surprisingly cool and dry, like tissue paper, and the thin fingers were bent. Meg tried not to think of the chicken's foot that one of the boys had swiped from the science room last year, but the image kept floating before her eyes.

"H-hello," was all she could think of to say. She felt like an idiot standing there, but Mim wouldn't let go of her hand.

"It's been close to seventy-five years since any children stayed in that house. How nice that there will be some now." The old woman released Meg's hand (finally!) and leaned back in her rocking chair. "Tell me about your family, child." Mim seemed to half close her eyes, but she kept smiling and started to rock the chair very slightly.

As Meg stumbled through a recitation of her family members, she found herself mesmerized by Talley's great-grandmother. How old could she be? She talked about seventy-five years ago like it was just yesterday. She had to be well over ninety. Meg had never seen anyone so old. Thin white hair was neatly arranged over the old lady's smooth pink scalp in a small bun at the back of her head. Her skin seemed thin, too. You could see the veins all squiggly and blue under it. In spite of the heat she wore a long-sleeved black dress with a little white collar, and the collar was pinned with a beautiful pin.

"Three boys and a girl. That's a lovely family," Mim exclaimed when Meg had finished. "Miss Rachel Rodgers of course never married, but I remember well when her nieces and nephews would come to visit and bring their children." Mim chuckled softly, almost to herself. " 'Mind you well, Alice Anne,' Miss Rachel used to say to me, 'Mind you well, that a house without children can never be called a home.' " Mim opened her eyes wide and stopped rocking. "It was not her fault, you know, that Miss Rachel never married. No indeed. It was not her fault at all. And it happened all too often to the young girls of marryin' age in Miss Rachel's day. That was a sad time. A very sad time."

Mim closed her eyes again for a moment, and with a small wave of her hand said, "I believe there are cookies in the jar, Talmadge. Good-bye, Meg Hamilton. I hope you'll come again and visit me sometime. We could have a good little chat. I'm very glad that you and your family are here." She seemed to stress the words "you and your family" and Meg wondered what the old woman meant by that.

With an uncomfortable smile to the old lady Meg followed Talley out of the room and into a large room that was the kitchen. Meg looked around in surprise. This room was as bright as the other room had been dark. The outside walls appeared to be white painted rock. "So this is in the stone part of the house," Meg thought. The white paint made even the storm's dim light appear bright and sunny. Light flowed in through a wide window over the kitchen sink, and in through a pair of French doors at the back of the room.

Everything in this room seemed to be old, too. A funny green- and cream-colored stove sat up on high legs, with a small oven next to the burners. Meg had never seen anything like it. The refrigerator was up on high legs, too, and was much smaller than their new model at home. In the middle of the room was a large round table surrounded by six yellow chairs. A curious-looking cabinet, with pieces of metal sheets imbedded in its doors, stood along one wall. The sheets had designs in them, circles and stars, made out of holes punched in the metal. There were blue and white bowls on top of the cabinet, and blue-and-white checked curtains at the window. Clay flowerpots held healthy-looking geraniums, blooming pink and white. It was all very simple, but it was a room that made you feel that you should just go in and sit down, as if you were welcome.

"Have a seat," Talley told her. He ducked into a door-way and returned with a big brown stoneware jar. "Cookies," he told her. "Gosh, I almost forgot about calling your mother. The telephone is over there on the wall."

Meg gave a guilty start. She had forgotten about calling home, too. Quickly she dialed their number, grateful that she had already memorized it.

"Hello," someone shouted into her ear. Good—it was Micah. She wouldn't have to talk to Mom yet. "Tell Mom I'm over at Talley Gradey's house, will you, Micah? No, I didn't get wet. Tell her I'll be home when the rain stops."

"Okay!" Micah yelled into the phone. "*P-chu P-chu P-chu! Rat-ta-ta-ta-tat!* Over and out!" Meg imagined that G.I. Joe was about to launch a new offensive. Micah was old enough to take a message; she just hoped he would remember to give it to Mom.

Talley was pouring two glasses of milk at the table. "Have a cookie. They're molasses raisin." He already had one stuffed in his mouth. Meg thought they sounded disgusting, but she took one to be polite. Her stomach growled, and she realized that she had stormed off to the barn without any lunch. The cookie was thick and soft, and when she bit into it she was surprised at how delicious it was. The flavor was rich and brown—sugary, old-fashioned, somehow, just like the house.

After she had eaten her second cookie Meg asked Talley to tell her about his house. "Is it very old?" she asked as she looked around again.

"Well, it is old for this part of the country." Talley tilted his head to one side and considered. "Mim should be the one to tell you about it. She was born here, and her great-grandfather built it. At least, he built the stone part. The log part is older. You'll have to come over sometime in the morning, and have a real visit. Mim usually is kind of sleepy in the afternoons, but she loves to have company."

That wasn't exactly what Meg had in mind. She was much too uncomfortable around Talley's great-grandmother to sit and have a real visit, as Talley put it. Meg didn't think she had ever been around anyone as old as Talley's Mim. It gave her the creeps! Her skin was so wrinkled and she was so tiny. What if she suddenly got sick (or even worse!) in the middle of their visit? What if she couldn't hear what Meg was saying? She seemed to hear okay, but everybody knew that old people were deaf. Maybe Meg should yell at her next time, just in case. "Or I could bring Micah with me," she thought, and almost giggled out loud.

"No, it's impossible," Meg told herself as she ate another cookie. "I've never been around old people. I'm not the type of person who can stand to be around them, that's all. No way I can sit and actually have a 'good chat' with that old lady."

Talley continued to eat cookies, first picking the raisins out and then cramming the whole thing in his mouth at once. He seemed perfectly happy, and oblivious of the fact that Meg was becoming impatient.

"Why can't *you* just tell me about this house?" she finally asked again.

Talley adjusted his glasses and brushed the remains of the last cookie from around his mouth. "I couldn't tell it like Mim." He gazed at her with his wide blue eyes and that choirboy expression she was beginning to find maddening. "Why not come over tomorrow?"

Meg answered him with another question. "You don't live here all alone with your grandmother, do you?"

"Great-grandmother," Talley corrected. "Of course not. My mother lives here, too. She's at work. She works at the Golden Lamb. In Lebanon." He noticed the blank look on Meg's face and patiently explained. "It's a restaurant, and a place to stay, but not like a motel. It's like an old-fashioned inn." He swiveled around in his chair and looked out the window. "Actually, it is an old inn. It's been there since the early 1800s."

"Why do you call your great-grandmother Mim?"

Talley set his glass of milk down on the table and pushed his glasses up on his nose. "Well, a long time ago, when Mim's first grandchild was little, he tried and tried to say 'Grandma,' but it kept coming out as 'Mim.' Everybody thought it was so funny, and Mim decided it's what she was meant to be called. It's what all her grandchildren and her great-grandchildren have called her ever since. Actually, it's what everybody calls her, now."

Meg had never heard of a grandmother being called Mim, but somehow it fitted the little old lady perfectly. "Are your parents divorced?" Meg asked. Since Talley hadn't mentioned a father, she figured that they must be. "No." Talley stared hard at the cookie in his hand. "My dad died of leukemia three years ago."

Meg felt her face flush and wished she had kept her mouth shut, but Talley jumped quickly to his feet and said, "Hey, the rain's stopped. You want to go outside?" He seemed perfectly normal.

Glad to change the subject, Meg pushed her chair back and stood up. "Yeah, but I think I'd probably better get home. Do you know what time it is?"

Talley pointed to the wall behind her, and the clock looked as old as everything else did in his house. "Almost six o'clock already! I really need to go!" Where had the time gone? She must have slept much longer than she realized up in the barn loft. "Can I just go out through these doors? Then I won't need to bother your grand— er—great-grandmother."

"Sure." Talley opened the French doors. "I'll walk you as far as the Big Oak." At Meg's questioning look he explained. "It's the oldest tree in the whole county, according to the state forestry people. It's sort of a landmark." And before Meg could protest, he started off across the wet grass.

The air was much cooler than it had been before the storm. The clouds had all blown themselves away, and the sky was a clear, pale blue. It seemed as if the storm had scrubbed the sky clean. Off in the distance thunder still rumbled faintly. Water dripped from the cabin's roof. A bird, a mourning dove, Talley told her, started to call. The sound was low and sad and indescribably lovely.

Before they reached the woods, a battered and faded yellow Volkswagen bug sputtered into view on the gravel lane and stopped in front of the house.

Talley turned back to the car. "Come back for a minute. You can meet my mother."

The woman in the Volkswagen got out, and Meg couldn't help but stare. Talley's mother was wearing a long blue dress with a white bibbed apron, and wore a ruffled white cap over her dark red hair.

She looked like a figure out of the past, a ghost, standing as she did in front of the old log-and-stone house. Only the presence of the little car gave an incongruous feel to the scene. Talley's mother waved to them and started across the lawn, holding her skirts up off the wet grass.

"Hey, Mom," Talley called as she approached. "This is Meg Hamilton, the girl I told you about."

By now Mrs. Gradey was close enough to reach out her hand. "I'm happy to meet you, Meg." She smiled warmly at Meg as she shook her hand. She had round blue eyes like Talley's, except that hers looked tired, and something else, Meg thought. Worried, maybe, or sad. She remembered what Talley said about his father.

"My mom wears a costume like this for her job at the Golden Lamb." Talley had noticed her staring.

Mrs. Gradey laughed. "I guess I do look a little strange. I manage the gift shop at the inn. We sell antique repro-ductions and crafts, and we all need to look in period. How do you like Ohio so far? Talley told me you're from Colorado."

"Um—it's a lot different," Meg said. It was all she could think of to say. She couldn't very well tell Talley's mother what she really thought.

"Yes, it is. I imagine you hate it right now, don't you? But give it a chance." She smiled warmly at Meg. "We're delighted your family got the Rodgers farm. I want to meet your mother and all those brothers real soon." She looked at Talley. "I'm going in to change. Supper in a half hour, okay?"

"I was just going to walk as far as the Oak," Talley told her. "Come on, Meg."

"Good-bye, Mrs. Gradey," Meg said, and she followed Talley across the grass to the path through the woods. "What a nice lady," Meg thought. The way she talked, it seemed as if she really knew how Meg was feeling about living in Ohio. At least someone understood how she felt. Too bad it had to be a stranger.

The path was wet, but not slippery. The thick canopy of leaves overhead had protected it from most of the rain. Water still dripped from the trees and everything smelled mossy, the way the colors green and brown would smell if they had a fragrance.

Meg thought about facing her mother again after the things she had said that afternoon. "Would Mom be mad?" she wondered. She hoped her mother had forgotten the whole thing. "I didn't really mean it when I said I hated her," Meg thought as she ducked her head beneath a low branch, "but I did mean what I said about moving here."

Somehow, though, the words sounded flat and empty in her head, as if she had gotten tired of thinking them. She didn't think about it long, anyway. She couldn't wait to tell her mother all about the house in the woods filled with old things, and especially about Mim.

Meg saw her father's car as soon as she turned the corner of the barn. She had hoped to get home before he did, to maybe have a chance to patch things up with her mother. "Oh, well," she thought with an air of resignation. "I guess things can't get a whole lot worse between me and my parents." She was sure that now, at least, she wouldn't go flying off the handle again. She felt too peaceful, all calm and quiet inside.

The lawn was littered with small twigs and leaves. The wind had blown a lot in the storm. Everything looked fresh and clean, as if the rain had washed away all the heat and dust of summer.

Her mother turned from the kitchen sink as Meg walked into the kitchen. "Hi, Meg." She gave a smile that said, "Don't worry about this afternoon. It's all forgotten and forgiven."

Meg returned the smile gratefully. Now everything seemed to be much better. It was as if the storm had cleaned and refreshed her, too.

Eagerly she told her mother about her visit to the funny little cabin she had discovered through the woods, about Talley's mother and great-grandmother.

"You have to go see it, Mom. It's the oldest-feeling place—it almost feels like a museum, but it's too lived in and homey for that." As she was talking, her father came in, dressed in a faded blue work shirt and jeans.

"And you have to go see the Big Oak. It's the oldest tree in the county, and it's on the state list of big trees."

She chattered on, setting the table for supper, oblivious of the worried look that passed between her parents.

—Four—

MEG ended up in charge of Micah and Daniel the next morning. Mom had shopping to do in Lebanon, and she planned to take the baby as well as Micah and Daniel, but the little boys complained.

"We don't want to leave here to go to the dumb old grocery store," Micah declared. "I've got a lot of exploring to do."

"Me, too," Daniel agreed gravely. "I need to th'plore with Micah." Sometimes Daniel could rattle off the longest scientific name imaginable, and then have trouble with common everyday words. "We're going withard hunting!" he continued. He meant lizard hunting.

"You don't mind, do you, Meg?" Mom asked. "I'll be gone no more than an hour and a half."

"I guess not," Meg answered. She might as well baby-sit, since there was nothing else to do. Back home things would have been different. If she was back home in Little-ton, she'd probably be at the mall with Alicia. Or she'd be at Heather's, splashing in her backyard swimming pool and working on a tan. Meg longed for that cool, blue water, and she missed the noisy, crowded shops of Buffalo Crossing Mall. The rage that once might have built up inside her did not materialize, but that old achy knot of loneliness and homesickness was back.

"I guess I'm getting used to it here," she thought, but the idea did not please her. "I don't want to get used to it, or grow to like it," she told herself. "This isn't where I belong, and it will never feel like home. At least I don't feel as strange here as I did at first." Not strange, just bored.

They waved, and Meg even managed to smile as the blue station wagon drove out the lane and down the road toward town. She turned to her brothers.

"Well, what do you want to do first?" she asked them.

"We don't need you around, Meg. We're just going exploring in the barn," Micah said in his best tough guy tone.

"Yeah," Daniel echoed importantly. It wasn't often that Micah allowed him to join in—only when there were no other kids around to play with—and Daniel was determined to make the most of this opportunity.

Meg hesitated. Mom didn't say she had to stick to the boys like glue. And, anyway, what kind of trouble could they possibly get into in the old barn?

"Okay. I'll be on the front porch, probably, or up in my room. Don't go anyplace but the barn. And be careful. Don't mess with anything you shouldn't."

The boys dashed off. Callahan appeared out of nowhere, and charged after them with a furiously wagging tail. He always seemed to know when an adventure was afoot, and never wanted to miss out on the action.

Meg stretched her arms over her head and gave a jaw-popping yawn. She was looking forward to being lazy this morning. She decided to go dig up a book, find the coolest, most comfortable place she could, and stay there until her mother got back from town.

Most of their family's books had already been unpacked—she had done it—and were in the tall oak cases in the front parlor. Meg scanned the familiar titles. Most of the books had been sitting on these same shelves for as long as she could remember, back in Littleton, and they felt like old friends.

She smiled to herself. That's exactly what she needed right now—an old friend.

There was the complete set of Shakespeare's works, many thick volumes with dark red leather covers and gilt printing: The histories, the tragedies, the comedies, the romances, the sonnets. She liked to hear Mom read the sonnets aloud, but she didn't understand them very well yet. The words had a wonderful sound, though, the way her mother read them. Even though Meg couldn't understand them, she could feel those poems, the way Mom read them.

She passed by her mother's other favorite poets, Tennyson and Robert Frost and that magnificent Welshman, Dylan Thomas. There was the tattered, slim volume of the poems of A. A. Milne, and the equally battered and well-read A Child's Garden of Verses by Robert Louis Stevenson.

Her fingers stopped on a book she hadn't even thought about in a long time, and had overlooked when she filled the bookshelves. Its calico-print cover was faded and a little torn, and the last time Mom had read it to her, she must have been about eight: *Hitty, Her First Hundred Years,* by Rachel Field. There was an old friend indeed.

Meg carried the book thoughtfully upstairs, trying to remember the story. Hitty was a doll who had quite an amazing number of travels and adventures over her long life. As she reached her hundredth birthday, she wrote her memoirs. Meg had to smile to herself. Hitty had traveled far from home, too. "Maybe it'll do me good to read about her," she thought. "We might have a lot in common."

She had lost all track of time, engrossed in her book, when she became aware of the noise. She sat up on her bed, listening intently. It was Micah, and he was yelling, no, he was screaming her name over and over again.

Meg was down the stairs and out the back door in seconds. Micah's voice was still now. Oh, God, she cried to herself, let them be in the barn. Now she saw in her mind all the terrible things that might have caused Micah to cry for her like that. . . . Daniel, crumpled and bleeding with the pitchfork he had fallen on still sticking out of him . . . Daniel, fallen through a rotten spot in the floor and lying unconscious on the lower level of the barn . . . "Stop it!" she told herself. Her stomach tightened in fear and she fought down panic.

She was almost to the barn when she saw the now familiar old bicycle that Talley Gradey rode. It was lying on its side, back wheel still spinning. Talley must have been riding by and heard Micah before she did.

She pulled the door open and ran inside. In an instant, she saw what the problem was, and her legs felt weak with relief.

Daniel was straddling one of the two huge beams that

ran across the barn's main room. He appeared to be stuck, and could go neither forward nor backward to get to the vertical post, or to the other wall with ladders to reach the floor. One look at his scared, white face and his little legs dangling over the fifteen feet or so of empty space to the floor made Meg realize that the situation, while not as horrible as she had imagined, was nevertheless serious to Daniel.

Micah and Talley were standing in the middle of the floor, right underneath him. Callahan sat on the floor, whimpering softly, and nervously lifting his front paws up and down. He gave a short bark when Meg came in that seemed to say, "So you're finally here, now do something!"

"Daniel can't get down," Micah cried unnecessarily.

"Meg, I'm th-thtuck." Daniel's voice, high and thin, quivered near tears.

"It's okay, Daniel. You only have to move backward a little bit, and you'll be able to climb down the ladder." Meg tried to sound confident and calm. Tonight they would all be able to laugh about this, she told herself.

"No, Meg. I mean I'm really thtuck. Thomething ith thticking into me. Into the back of my leg. Meg, it hurth." He ended with a whimper that was not quite crying, trying very hard to be brave.

Meg looked at Talley. He stood on the floor, looking up at Daniel like the rest of them, hands stuffed deep into the pockets of his jeans. He looked as if he had all the calm and confidence that Meg was desperately trying to summon.

"What should we do?" she asked him. She realized that since he lived in the country he was much better acquainted with barns than she was.

"I think the best thing to do would be for you to climb

up and get behind him. I'll climb up the other side and walk over until I'm in front of him. With the two of us up there with him, maybe he'll feel more secure." He spoke quietly, and his idea sounded like a good one to Meg. She was glad that Talley had suggested she go up behind Daniel. She would only have to crawl several feet out onto the beam, while Talley had to climb the ladder against the wall and cross the whole width of the barn.

Daniel was crying softly now. "His leg must really hurt," Meg thought. "We're coming up, Daniel. Talley and I. Don't worry, we'll get you down." She talked to him the whole time she climbed the ladder and inched out onto the beam. When she was behind him, she looked up to see Talley carefully walking the beam toward them.

Talley deftly dropped down and straddled the beam in front of Daniel, who had managed to stop crying. His little face was white, tear-streaked, with red blotches. Meg's heart went out to him.

"Okay, let's see how you're stuck, Daniel." Meg reached her arms around her brother.

"No!" Daniel screamed. "Don't pull me! It hurth, Meg. I'm caught on a thticker!"

"He must mean a splinter," Talley said. "Daniel, can you take your hand off the beam and show me where you're stuck? Meg and I will hold you. We won't let you fall." Talley talked to him gently, but not like he was a little kid. He kept his voice low and calm.

Daniel's hands were clinging tightly to the beam, but slowly he lifted one and pointed to a spot on his right thigh. Meg shuddered to imagine the splinter he could have gotten from the old wood. It was roughly hewn and the surface was digging into her own bare legs uncomfortably as she sat on the beam.

"I'm thtickered right under here," Daniel said. He hiccuped, and swallowed hard, gulping back his tears.

"Okay, Daniel. You're doing great. Listen, Danny, were you crossing over to the wall when you got stuck?" Talley continued in a soft and friendly tone. The little blond head nodded. Talley looked over Daniel to Meg.

"Okay, we'll have to get him to move backward toward you to get himself off the splinter."

Meg started to question why, but suddenly understood what Talley meant. If Daniel had been inching himself forward over the beam, a splinter would have gone into him from the front, and the best way to get him off it would be to back him up, just the way he had come.

Meg shot Talley an admiring look. That was smart thinking. "I was just going to grab Daniel's leg and give it a little tug," she thought ruefully.

"All right, now, Danny, I want you to put your hands around my neck, and try to let your arms and legs get nice and loose and relaxed, okay?" Talley had Daniel's confidence. "Now, when we count to three, and it's very important that you help me count, nice and loud, Meg's going to pull you back a little bit, and you'll be pulled right off that old splinter. Now, here's what we're going to say— one, two, three, ouchy ouchy ouchy! Just like that, real fast and louder each time you say ouchy, okay?"

"Okay." Daniel almost giggled. Talley had him all calmed down, in just a few minutes.

"Great." Talley shot Meg a look. "You ready?"

Meg nodded. They didn't want to have to try this

twice. If they couldn't get Daniel off the first time, they might not be able to calm him down again. And there was a chance that all of them could lose their balance and fall.

"Okay, Danny, let's hear you count with me." Talley smiled at him. Together the two voices rose, Daniel's high and squeaky, but loud.

"One—two—three—ouchy—ouchy—*ouchy!*"

On the last and loudest "ouchy" Meg lifted her brother back toward her, as smoothly and as quickly as she could manage, balanced as they were on a sixteen-inch-wide beam fifteen feet above the ground.

Daniel yelled, but it was over so fast that it didn't have time to hurt much.

"I'm unthtickered!" he announced with surprise.

"I told you we'd get you off, didn't I?" Talley grinned. "Now Meg, just work your way back to the post, and down the ladder, and I'll stay right in front of you both."

They got to the ground without a mishap, and Meg had a chance to look at the back of Daniel's leg. Micah bent to look, too. The wound made by the splinter was about an inch long, but it was bleeding only a little, and it looked as though it was clean.

"I think the splinter's all out, don't you?" she asked Talley. He examined the wound closely and nodded his head in agreement.

"Your mom will be able to fix it right up, won't she, Danny?" Usually Daniel had a fit when anyone called him Danny.

"I think tho, with a Band-Aid." Daniel wasn't nearly so white anymore, and he managed a shaky smile as he looked up at his rescuer.

"Don't you two go climbing around the barn with shorts on, okay?" Talley's stern look took in Micah, too. "And never, ever with bare feet."

"We won't," the two little boys spoke together. They looked at Talley with something close to hero worship in their eyes.

Talley and Meg followed the boys up to the house. "Thanks for your help, Talley. I don't think I could have gotten him down without you." Meg really meant it. What had looked like a laughable situation at first could have been a tragedy if Daniel had fallen.

"I'm glad I was riding by," Talley answered.

"You knew just how to handle Daniel up there on that beam." She hated to admit it, even to herself, but Talley had really saved Daniel from at best, a traumatic experience, and at worst—well, Meg hated to think what could have happened. And all while she was in charge of the boys.

They were on the front porch drinking lemonade when the station wagon drove up. Mom beeped the horn and waved gaily. Micah and a totally recovered, iodined, and Band-Aided Daniel ran around the corner of the house to tell their mother all about the morning's adventure.

"Thank goodness it had a happy ending," Meg thought again. The boys had certainly found a new friend. Talley had promised to take them hunting for crayfish in the creek. And Meg had invited him to eat lunch with them. It just seemed the right thing to do, after he practically saved Daniel's life.

She had to admit to herself that she had been a little— well, more than a little, wrong about Talley Gradey.

— Five —

MIM'S dark eyes sparkled even in the shadowy light of the log cabin's living room. "Actually," Talley pointed out, "this room was the first part of the house to be built. For a while it was kitchen, living room, and bedroom. But we just call it the old kitchen. You can see the brick oven built into the side of the fireplace. We still use it in the winter."

Meg listened to him with a polite look on her face, but her thoughts were far from polite. "I can't believe I agreed to come over here," she thought bleakly to herself. She felt so uncomfortable in Talley's great-grandmother's presence. Was it possible that Mim knew what she was thinking, that the old lady thought it amusing to watch her squirm? Meg decided she had never been looked over so completely or so thoroughly by anyone before. Mim's eyes almost disappeared in her wrinkled face when she smiled, but the look she gave Meg seemed to bore right through her.

Meg shifted her thin china teacup from one hand to the other. It felt funny to have a dress on in the middle of the week in the summer, but her mother had insisted. "How nice to be invited for afternoon tea. Of course you'll wear a dress." Meg couldn't help feeling that the whole idea was dumb, but somehow she couldn't refuse when Talley invited her. She kept remembering how great he had been with Daniel in the barn. Now she was wishing she had made up some excuse to stay away.

"How do you like the tea?" Talley asked, and Meg realized she hadn't tasted it yet. Quickly she took a sip, and her eyes flew open in surprise at the strong flavor. It was minty—and something else.

"It's very good," she said. "What is it?"

"It is our favorite kind," Mim answered. "Black peppermint and lemon verbena. We grow it in the garden, and harvest it during the summer and dry enough of it to last all year long."

Meg took another sip. She had seen her mother buy herb tea in the grocery store. "We have mint growing by our barn," she told Mim. "I don't know what kind it is, but do you think we could make tea out of that?"

"Of course," the old lady answered. "That's black peppermint, too, taken from the beds here when the Rodgers moved over to the big house. It was planted around the stone foundation wall of the barn in 1836 or thereabouts." She paused for a second and gave Meg a knowing look. " 'Course, *I* don't remember it, but that's what my grandma told me." Mim's eyes twinkled mischievously.

"Cut the mint in the morning," Mim continued, still smiling, "but only after the dew has dried. Tie the stems together in bunches, and hang the bunches upside down in an airy kind of place to dry. When 'tis dry, strip the leaves off the stems and there you have your tea. We save bundles of the dried stems to use as kindling in the fireplace. Smells mighty nice, like summer in the dead of winter."

"Meg, try some shortbread." Talley passed her a plate. "My mother tries and tries to make shortbread as good as Mim's, but she never has yet."

"Oh, you are mistaken there, Talmadge. It's every bit as good as mine."

Talley's great-grandmother made these delicate, buttery cookies? Meg couldn't believe it. She hardly looked able to totter around a kitchen. "I've been wrong about Mim," Meg realized. "She's not nearly as decrepit as I thought." In spite of herself, Meg began to relax, and leaned back in her chair. Mim poured out more tea, and Meg looked at the pretty china and glass vase full of flowers on the small round table.

"Did you grow those flowers in the garden here, too?"

"No, child. Those are wildflowers, that grow in the woods and fields hereabouts. Talley can show you where to find them."

Meg leaned over to look closer at the bouquet. The flowers were smaller and more delicately colored than the flamboyant blooms of cultivated plants. "These all grow around here?" she asked.

"Sure. All over the place," Talley said. "Mim can tell you all about them. Some of them have great stories and lots of uses."

Meg fingered a lacy, white, flat flower head about three inches across. "What's this one called?"

"That's Queen Anne's lace," Mim said. "Lovely, isn't it? In olden times they grated the root and put it on burns.

Very soothing, it was. See the one dark floweret in the center? Well, the story goes that Queen Anne was making lace, and pricked her finger with the needle. That one flower represents the drop of blood that fell on the lace."

"Is there always just one dark flower in the center?" Meg asked.

"Always," Mim replied. She put one thin, bent finger on a tiny, dark blue flower with a yellow center. "This one's story goes like this: Two young lovers were walking along a fast-moving river when the girl spied this pretty little flower. The boy leaned over to pick it for her, but when he did, he slipped and fell right into the river. As the swift current carried him away he threw his love the flower, and cried, 'Forget me not!' "

"Forget-me-nots!" Meg exclaimed in delight. "I've heard of those!"

"They grow in moist places, like along streams," Talley grinned. "Just like in Mim's story."

"Only trouble with these little blooms is they don't last long. Only a day or so," Mim said. "We only pick a few for special occasions, don't we, Talmadge? Wildflowers are not so common as they once were."

It made Meg feel good to know that having her over for tea was a special occasion. She thought about it later as she walked back on the path along the creek—the Little Peavine. She had thought Talley an idiotic little kid, and she was wrong about that. And she had been frightened of Mim because she was so very old. She thought Mim was beyond talking to—too old to hear or see or remember anything. It looked as though she was wrong about that, too. Still, she wished Mim wasn't quite so old, so shriveled and frail. Meg wondered if she'd ever feel comfortable around the old lady.

That evening was Micah's night to clear the table and dry, and Meg's job to wash. She preferred it that way. Micah meant well, but he didn't get the dishes very clean when he washed. She sometimes had to wash them over.

Dad came through the kitchen with Nicholas in the backpack carrier. "You two almost done?" he asked. "Mom and Daniel and I are going for a walk. Want to come, Meg? Micah?"

"I'd like to stay here, Dad. Thanks, anyway."

"I'm meeting Chad and some other kids to play baseball in Mr. Ryan's old cornfield, Dad. They play every night after supper, and guess what! They even said Cal could play!" Micah almost dropped a glass he was trying to dry in his excitement at the thought of the game.

"Callahan is a pretty good outfielder," Dad said, and smiled.

"Here, Micah. Give me that glass before you break it," Meg said. "I'll finish drying for you. Go play ball." Anything was better than G.I. Joe.

The screen door slammed and Micah dashed down the steps with his glove and bat, Callahan so close behind him that he almost lost his footing.

"That was sweet of you, Meg." Dad looked at her thoughtfully. "Things are getting easier for you here, aren't they?"

"I guess so," Meg admitted. She swirled the dishcloth through the sudsy water in the sink. "I guess I'm getting used to this place, but that kind of scares me."

"I think I understand," Dad said. "It's hard to let go of things that we're used to, isn't it? But that's what life is all about. It changes all the time, and we constantly adjust and change and grow with it."

"I feel like I'm forgetting my friends, though."

"You aren't being disloyal to your old friends by learning to make new ones, you know."

"I don't feel like Denver's home anymore, but I don't feel like Ohio's home, either."

"I know. Just give it time."

They heard Daniel clatter down the stairs, and Mom call after him, "Daniel, slow down!"

Dad smiled at Meg and gave her a quick hug. "Know what I think?" Meg shook her head. "I think you're growing up." Meg hugged him back and smiled, but she wasn't so sure.

After her family left, the kitchen was unusually quiet. Meg scrubbed out the sink and wiped off the counters and the table.

As she picked up the glass jar with her brother's crayfish inside, she found herself thinking about Talley's house. Everything in it, each piece of furniture, seemed to fit in so perfectly, as though it had always belonged there. Mim seemed to fit in there, too, maybe because she was so old. But Talley and his mother seemed to fit in in the same way.

It was funny. She couldn't seem to get Talley's great-grandmother out of her mind. She was fascinated by Mim but also a little repulsed. How old could Mim be, anyway? Maybe close to a hundred years old—a whole century. Meg looked at her hands as she dried them off and hung up the towel. Smooth thirteen-year-old hands. She squirted some lotion on them from a container her mother kept by the sink. As she rubbed it in, she saw again Mim's tiny, bent fingers and felt their papery dryness. It was hard to imagine that Mim's hands had ever looked like hers, but of course they had once. It was harder still to think that someday, if Meg lived to be a very old woman, her hands would be changed and look like Mim's. Changing. Was it all a part of life, like Dad said?

The time she had spent with Mim and Talley this afternoon had turned out to be much better than she had imagined it would. The stories Mim told about the wild-flowers were fascinating. "Maybe it would be fun to really explore the woods and creek to see how many different kinds I could find," Meg decided to herself. It would be fun to make a collection; to learn as much as she could about the subject. "I bet that's something I could do," she thought, "something I could be good at." She hummed to herself as she put the last dishes up in the cupboard.

After all her chores were done in the kitchen, Meg walked aimlessly through the house. Everything was so still with her brothers gone. It was only the second time she had been in the house all by herself, and it gave her a queer feeling, almost as though she was snooping through a stranger's house. She walked about the rooms, and it was as if she were seeing them for the first time. Was Dad right? Would this strange place ever seem familiar?

The kitchen was big enough to eat in, with old-fashioned glass-doored cupboards hanging on the walls, and a huge old white porcelain sink. Her parents planned to remodel it next summer. It was one of the things that could wait awhile on the house. Meg knew that carpenters had worked for several weeks before the family moved in, doing the major repairs that were needed. Plumbers had modernized the two bathrooms, which Dad said was a real necessity with four children.

The house had been built ages ago—Meg didn't know for sure how old it was, but she thought it must be well over a hundred years. Her parents had been thrilled to find it, that was all she really knew. It had been rented to the same farmer and his wife for the last thirty-odd years, and had stood vacant for some time before the Hamiltons bought it.

She stood in the front hall for a few minutes, just looking around, making a conscious effort to feel comfortable in the house.

Finally she turned back into the kitchen and poured herself a glass of lemonade. Breaking the rule about no food upstairs, she carried it up to her bedroom. She turned slowly all the way around. No, it just didn't look right, and it certainly didn't feel right. She gazed at it critically for a few minutes, but couldn't decide what the problem was. Her bed was piled with her collection of teddy bears, and the low bookshelf Dad had made for her was under one of the windows, just like in her old room back in Littleton. Jemima, the tabby cat, looked up from the cushion where she had been napping, and meowed. Meg dropped down on the floor beside her and gathered the cat into her lap.

"Jemima, do *you* feel at home here?" Sometimes cats and dogs had a hard time adjusting to new surroundings. Jemima stretched and purred loudly. She didn't seem to be in the least way unadjusted. Of course, she had not been happy about the car trip from Colorado, but as soon as they let her out of the carrier, she was fine. And Callahan, the big goof, seemed to be happier than ever, running around the fields and sleeping in the shade of the big maple trees.

"You're a traitor, too!" she muttered into the cat's soft fur. Even the family's pets had deserted her. Was she the only one to feel lonely and out of place here? Nobody else seemed to miss malls and stores, friends and mountains and sky. She put Jemima back down on the cushion. "Traitor," she muttered to the cat again. Jemima acted as though she hadn't even heard, curled up in her favorite impossible-looking position, and went back to sleep.

Meg sat on her bed and looked around. She thought about Talley's strange little house. Everything seemed to belong there, and nothing seemed to belong here, especially Meg herself. That old familiar knot tightened in her chest.

She tried to make herself feel angry, but she just couldn't seem to do it. Dad was probably right. And, anyway, a reasonable voice said in her head, look how wrong you were about Talley. He had been great out in the barn with Daniel. The boys had had a marvelous time roaming up and down the creek with him all afternoon, and so, Meg had to admit to herself, had she.

Talley showed them all sorts of tiny creatures that lived in the creek. Things like round, transparent water pennies, and the nifty little houses that caddis fly larvae build out of pebbles. They found a particularly nasty-looking creature Talley called a hellgrammite. Meg shivered at the memory of the pinchers the thing had, but her brothers were fascinated by it.

They had even found some wildflowers, and Meg brought a few home and pressed them in between two pieces of tissue paper and tucked them in the middle of one of the volumes of Shakespeare. She would have to get Mim to identify them for her; they were the first specimens of her wildflower collection. She thought she might even attempt some rough pencil sketches of the plants.

She searched in a drawer for paper, found some, but then could find no pencil. Frustrated, she slammed the drawer shut, then paced around her room, feeling restless. Finally, she left her sweating glass of lemonade on a paperback book on the dresser and went down the hall past the bathroom and the other bedrooms.

She stopped in front of the door to the attic. This would be the perfect chance to explore. The door stuck a little as she opened it, as if it hadn't been used very much. She had never been up there, in the old third-floor attic, but she couldn't imagine her parents minding if she looked around. There was a light switch on the wall, but when she turned it on, no light appeared. She clicked it back and forth a few times, and in the end decided that either the bulb was burned out or the wiring had gone bad.

"It's probably a good thing not to use the electric light, anyway," Meg thought as she climbed the steep, dusty stairs in near darkness. Groping in the dark made it feel more like she was doing something she shouldn't, made the trip to her own attic feel like an adventure. Their house in Littleton had no real attic—just an empty space between rafters and roof with a fold-down ladder and a tiny trapdoor in the ceiling.

At the top of the stairs she stood still, looking around her and giving her eyes a chance to adjust to the gloom. There were four small windows, but the meager light they let in left large areas of spooky darkness and shadows. Gradually, as her eyes became used to the light, Meg could make out interesting shapes—piles of boxes and some bulky things covered with sheets.

Meg shivered with a delicious feeling of excitement, of anticipation, and the hair stood up on her arms and on the back of her neck.

One time, back in Littleton, she and Alicia had spent an hour digging around in Alicia's older sister's room, and had gotten in terrible trouble for it. But snooping, while not very honorable maybe, was always great fun, and as she turned and went back down the steps as quickly as she dared for her flashlight, she was smiling.

Six

THE beam from the flashlight flickered over the darker corners of the attic. She saw a birdcage and an old Christmas tree stand, two kerosene lanterns covered with cobwebs, and a broken chair. The attic was still hot from the heat of the day, and smelled dusty and stale.

Gingerly, with just the tips of her fingers, she pulled at the nearest sheet, afraid of spiders. The only motion was the cloud of dust she disturbed. Relieved, but still wary, Meg opened the box on top: record albums, with titles like *Christmas with Tennessee Ernie Ford* and *The Best of the Lennon Sisters*. She flipped through them quickly and went on to the next box. It was filled with a set of ugly green plastic dishes and a flowered plastic tablecloth with a hole in the middle of it. The box on the bottom held five saucepans of different sizes, all dented and dull, some old spoons, and one rubber boot.

Meg shook her head and her forehead creased in a disappointed frown. There certainly wasn't much to get excited about. Still, she continued to poke through the attic. It looked as if the stuff was exactly what Dad said it was, just old junk. And not too old, either. Only worthless stuff from the fifties and sixties, it looked like. The house hadn't been lived in since then, she guessed. She passed by a floor lamp with no shade, and an ugly clock with a bright red rooster on it.

She had worked her way to the very darkest corner of the attic when she saw it. It was covered with a faded pink blanket, and there was a toaster and a broken basket on top of it, but right away she knew she had found something special. The feeling flooded through her in a rush of excitement. The flashlight's beam rested on one partially exposed end, and the reddish-colored wood glowed in its feeble light.

Carefully Meg removed the toaster and basket, not even thinking about spiders. The satin binding of the blanket caught on a corner, and she spent some time loosening it. She pulled the cover off, and stood staring at what she had found.

It was a chest, with simple but beautiful lines. It looked handmade and very old. The wood was smooth as silk, with a lovely color that was warm and deep even in the dim light of the attic. It was about four feet long, and maybe half that deep and tall.

She crouched next to it and ran her hand along the top. That was when she saw the date carved into the side. 1774. She closed her eyes and shook her head, thinking that she was mistaken, but when she opened her eyes again the date was still there.

Meg realized she had been holding her breath, and let it out with a long, ragged noise. She sat back on her heels a little, to get a better view of the front of the chest. There was more carving—two sets of initials, and a heart encircling the letters and date. The heart was formed of delicate vines with tiny leaves and flowers. There were even several small birds in among the leaves of the vine. Whoever had carved it had spent a lot of time on this chest, Meg could tell. She touched it again lightly, following the lines of the carving with the tips of her fingers. She had never touched anything so old before.

She didn't know how long she sat there, but suddenly, from far below her, she heard the back door slam and feet pound across the kitchen floor. Meg jumped to her feet and covered the chest again so that none of it showed. As quietly as she could, she went down the attic stairs. She held her breath as she opened the door, but this time it didn't stick. She was able to close it without a sound, and by the time the boys came running upstairs, she was lying on her bed with her radio on and a book in her hands. When her brothers came in to tell her about their walk and the baseball game, they didn't notice that her book was upside down.

She wasn't sure why she didn't want her family to know about what she had found in the attic. Of course she would tell them about it eventually, but for a little while she wanted it to be hers, just hers.

The sun was shining the next morning when Meg awoke. The leaves of the big gnarled apple tree right outside her windows made a moving pattern of shadows on the old-fashioned shades. She didn't get up right away, but lay there, looking at the flowers on her wallpaper, and thinking about the same things that had kept her awake the night before. Who had built the chest? How did it get in the attic of their house? And was there anything inside?

Meg would have to wait to open the chest. She didn't want her sometimes pesky little brothers around, or even her parents, when she did. This was her discovery, hers all alone. She imagined what archaeologists must have felt like just before they opened the tomb of an ancient Egyptian king. She remembered seeing a *National Geographic* special about finding old shipwrecks in the ocean. Those treasure hunters couldn't have felt much different than she did. She would wait until she was alone again in the house, or at least until everyone in her family was busy with something else. She shivered with excitement and a delicious feeling of anticipation. She could hardly wait for the chance to see what was in the chest.

She didn't have to be patient very long. As she finished her bowl of cereal that very morning her mother announced a trip into town.

"Nicholas will be due for a booster shot next month, so I made an appointment to meet the pediatrician in town," Mom told her. "I'm taking the boys to meet her, too. And if you'd like to come that would be great. We're going to meet Dad and have lunch at McDonald's." Mom smoothed Meg's hair and gave her a hug. "We'd love for you to come, but I know that you like to be home without such a big crowd around. Three little brothers can be just too many sometimes."

Meg gave her mother a grateful look. "I do like to be alone sometimes," she said. "Thanks, Mom. I would rather stay home." Maybe Mom understood her more than she thought. "And, um, about the other day," Meg felt compelled to say it, "I'm sorry I said those things to you. I didn't mean it."

"I know that, Meg. We all say things we don't mean at times. The important thing is to realize we don't really mean them." Her mother gave her a hug, and Meg returned the squeeze. "Hey, how would you like us to bring you a Big Mac and fries for lunch?"

"And a Coke?"

"And a Coke." Mother and daughter grinned at each other and then laughed when they both said "I love you" at the same time. Later Meg realized it had been a long time since she had said that to either of her parents. It felt good to say it, and Meg sang as she cleaned up her breakfast dishes.

She figured she would have at least two hours all alone in the house. That would be plenty of time to see what was in the chest. She was worried about the batteries in her flashlight, so she got one of the tall silver candlesticks from the mantel in the dining room and some matches from the kitchen, just in case.

The attic looked just the same as it had last night, but it felt different because now it was hers. Her attic, and her discovery. She walked straight to the corner that held the chest, took off the pink blanket, and dropped it on the floor out of the way. Then she went to the closest window, and with a lot of effort was able to turn the lock and open it. The old wood groaned in protest, but she was able to raise it all the way. Fresh morning air rushed into the stuffy attic.

"There, that's better, and I'll be able to hear the car

when Mom and the boys come home, too," she thought. "Everything's got to be perfect when I open the secret treasure chest."

She tried to prop the flashlight against the old toaster, but the results weren't right. The narrow beam of light only illuminated a small portion of the attic. In the end she lighted the candle, and placed it on a cracked wooden stool she found against a far wall. The candlelight was perfect. It wavered in the slight breeze from the open window and cast fantastic shadows on the walls behind her. It seemed right to use candlelight at the opening of the chest, she decided. Maybe the person who made it had worked on it by candlelight, back in 1774.

Meg stood in front of the chest and wiped her hands on the front of her shorts. She felt nervous, and the picture jumped into her mind of all the junk she had looked through in the attic. What if the chest contained more of the same? "It probably does," she told herself practically. "But it can't," another voice seemed to cry inside her. "It's such a beautiful thing! I know there's something special in it!"

Quickly she placed her hands under the edge of the top, and lifted. At the same time she closed her eyes and whispered, "Please, oh please! Let there be something wonderful inside! And don't let it be locked!"

The lid offered no resistance, and came up as if it might have been opened only yesterday. She opened her eyes, and stood staring down. After a long moment Meg sank to her knees on the floor in front of it.

She wrinkled up her nose and made a face. The smell that rose from the chest was musty, acrid, and unpleasant. It stung her eyes and caught in her throat until she coughed.

It was the smell that very old things acquire when they've been put away for years and years. To Meg it seemed a sad smell—the smell of neglect, of things forgotten.

The first thing she took out was a length of pale blue wool. It was fringed on both ends, and as she held it up and away from her she recognized it as a shawl. It was loosely woven, so that it would be soft but at the same time warm. "Mom will be interested in this," she thought. She folded the shawl and put it down on top of the pink blanket to protect it from dust.

She lifted out two quilts made from many different little scraps of material. Meg had seen quilts at the Colorado State Fair, but nothing like these. Most of the colors were faded blues and browns, and a rusty color that might have once been red. The pieces of material were very small. Hundreds of scraps must have been used. There were many patterns of flowers and dots and stripes, and the pieces had been quilted around the edges with the tiniest of stitches. The quilts were heavy, and she didn't take the time to unfold them, but put them on the blanket with the shawl.

She reached back into the chest, and hesitated a moment.

"Oh, baby clothes!" she cried softly. The little pile of clothing had been carefully folded and there were some dried leaves tucked in among them that crumbled when Meg touched them. The material was light and thin, and the workmanship was beautiful. The dresses were tucked and pleated, and each one had a narrow edging of rather coarse-looking lace and a row of tiny, roughly shaped buttons. The old material had once been white, but age had yellowed it to a soft cream color. There were dresses, and tiny shirts, and two small cap-shaped bonnets decorated with rosettes of ribbon.

There was another quilt underneath the baby clothes, a pattern of just blue and white. Each blue square had triangles sewed to two sides to make a design. The quilt underneath it was the fanciest. On a white background were intertwining rings made up of small pieces of fabric, their colors as bright as the day it had been made. "Maybe this quilt had never been used, but just kept put away in the chest," Meg thought. The whole surface was covered with the same tiny stitches, in a design of fanlike feathers. Even to Meg, who knew very little about sewing, it looked like a work of art.

Tucked into one corner of the chest was a packet of stiff canvas about the size of a paperback book. Meg almost overlooked it. The cord that tied it up was stubborn. When she finally undid the knot and unwrapped the cover she quickly dismissed the contents. "Just a bunch of old letters and stuff." She'd hoped it was jewelry or money—something really valuable. The papers were old and brittle, and the writing was faint and strange-looking, so Meg didn't bother to look through the stack. She tied it back up and put it on top of the pink blanket.

A folded piece of ivory-colored linen was the next thing she took out. When unfolded, it was about sixteen inches square.

"Oh my gosh!" she whispered. "It's a sampler!" It looked very familiar to her, and she remembered she had seen ones like it in her mother's textiles books. It was a sort of a practice piece, where the maker could try out different embroidery stitches. Sometimes the person who made the sampler even put her name and the date she worked on it.

Meg held the linen close to the candle. There were rows of flowers, and the alphabet and numbers up to ten, all sewn in colors that had once been as bright as her mother's wools downstairs. Now, they were faded to mostly browns and tans, with some still-dark greens and blues. The hundreds of little stitches were beautiful. There was a house flanked by two trees, and a horse and a cow. Underneath the house, Meg read the following:

Worked by Sarah Randall
in the Year of our Lord 1786,
in the tenth Year of her Age.

Sarah Randall, a girl younger than Meg was now, had made this lovely thing. Meg thought how hopelessly tangled her impatient attempts at sewing had been. How could anyone have the patience to do it? Meg smoothed the linen square on her lap. The animals on it were too large in comparison to the house, but the design was well thought out. She turned the sampler over, and the back of it was almost as neat as the front.

Almost reluctantly she put the sampler down and returned to the chest. From the bottom she lifted out a bulky bundle, wrapped in a length of yellowed linen. She unwrapped it on her knees. The linen, soft as butter with age, fell away to reveal a jacket made of blue material.

The blue of the coat was as dark as the darkest blue jeans. The wool fabric was stiff and thick. Meg could see that it was a military jacket of some kind. There was no insignia or gold braid, only a red collar and cuffs, and flat metal buttons that were dark gray with tarnish. She held the jacket out at arm's length by its shoulders. It seemed so small. Her father could not wear it, she was certain. Maybe it had been a play soldier jacket that a boy had worn. "I guess boys have always liked to play army, like Micah and his G.I. Joe men," she thought.

Whoever had worn it had used it a lot. There were several tears and worn places in the coat that had been carefully mended. Meg gently folded the coat back up and placed it back in the chest. Her hands felt dry and dirty and she was full of the smell of the quilts and clothes. The greatness of the discovery she had made was too much to absorb all at once. She felt almost as though she were dreaming as she put the things away. When she picked up the blanket to cover the chest, the packet of papers slid off unnoticed. She spread the tattered pink blanket (how soft and new it felt!), blew out the candle, and went downstairs, almost in a daze.

—Seven—

SAMPLER, jacket, quilts, and baby dresses whirled around in her head. She let the cold water in the bathroom sink pour over her hands and arms. She could still smell the musty odor from the chest. It clung to her clothes, her hair, inside her nose.

Suddenly, she had to be outside, in the open. Barely stopping to dry her arms and hands, she ran out of the bathroom and down the stairs. The back door slammed behind her and her tennis shoes pounded across the porch and down the brick walk. She didn't stop running until she reached the stream behind the barn.

It was much cooler than the last few days had been. The sky was blue, not as blue as the sky in Colorado, but blue nonetheless, with huge puffs of white cloud. In the shade of the trees it was pleasantly cool. Meg jumped the stream and sat under Talley's Big Oak.

She settled herself between two huge roots that had just enough space for her body, leaned her back against the rough bark of the tree, and gazed out toward their barn.

She was able to sit there comfortably in the deep shade of the woods and survey the bright sunshiny world of the pasture. Insects hummed in the grass—it was the only noise she heard. Out in the pasture, a half dozen white butterflies floated over the daisies sprinkled among the grass. The Little Peavine just beside her bubbled over the rocks.

She breathed deeply, catching her breath after the run from the attic. The air was full of the herby smell of leaves and grass and moss. It was wonderful to get the smell of the old cloth out of her nose. She lifted her hair up off her neck and then dropped her arms to her lap.

What had occupied her for the past hour or so seemed almost to be unreal, a dream. "I didn't imagine the whole thing, did I?" she wondered. Questions whirled through her mind. What hands had made those quilts? Who had worn the little baby dresses? Who had built the chest, for that matter, and who had worn that coat? Had it been for Sarah Randall's brother, or for someone only fifty years ago? She wasn't sure how old any of the things were, except the chest itself and the dated sampler.

"I've got to find out," she thought, "but where do I begin?" She answered her own question almost immediately. "I've got to talk to Talley Gradey's great-grandmother." She hated the thought, but she knew Mim was the only place, and maybe the best place, to start. She was probably the only person still around who remembered the people who had lived in the Hamiltons' house long ago, people named Rodgers.

Slowly she got up from the place between the tree roots and brushed off the seat of her shorts. She wondered what time it was, and decided she'd better check in at the house. She didn't want to be gone when her mother got back from town. This time she walked back to the house, through the pasture and around the side of the barn. Her eye caught a small reddish brown blur and she froze. A chipmunk held stone-still for a long moment and then flitted over the stone foundation and disappeared into a crevice.

Seeing the tiny animal made Meg feel ridiculously happy, and she danced the rest of the way up the drive just as her mother's blue station wagon pulled in.

Nicholas had fallen asleep and was slumped over with his cheek smashed against the side of his car seat. Daniel was heavy eyed, and even Micah seemed to be in a sleepy stupor after their busy morning. Mom waved at Meg and cut the engine. While she gathered up her purse and undid her seat belt, Meg opened the back door and quietly lifted her baby brother from his seat.

"I'll take him up to his crib," she whispered to her mother.

"Great," Mrs. Hamilton whispered back. "Then come down to the kitchen for your lunch." She held up the bag from McDonald's. "We've had a big morning. Come on, Micah, and you too, Daniel. I want you to have a rest, too." For once the boys didn't protest, but followed their mother quietly up the walk to the back porch.

When Meg came downstairs her mother was in the kitchen unloading a sack of groceries. "What did you do with yourself this morning?" she asked as Meg came in.

"Oh, nothing much." Meg couldn't share her secret yet. Pretending to be interested in groceries, she put two boxes of macaroni and cheese in a cupboard, and reached back into the sack for a box of Cheerios. "I read for a while and then I took a walk across the stream." A note of excitement crept into her voice. "Mom, did you know there are chipmunks here? I saw one by the barn."

"Are there? Oh, I love chipmunks! Remember how much fun they were to watch up in the mountains?"

"Remember when we heard them sliding on the roof of our tent early in the morning?" Meg grinned. "I never knew they did anything like that."

"And they came right up to us for crusts of bread."

Meg stopped unloading groceries. Here they were, talking about times in Rocky Mountain National Park, and she wasn't upset. It was a wonderful memory, but even thinking about it a couple of weeks ago would have made Meg dissolve into tears. She remembered what Dad had said about life and changes, adjusting and growing. "Yeah, maybe I am growing up," she decided.

Dinner had been over for a long time, and the little boys were in bed. They sat on the wide front porch in the fading light. A slight breeze helped cool the evening, and fireflies worked their magic over the lawn and in the field across the road. The first stars hung in the darkening sky.

"I don't think I'll ever get tired of watching this," her mother said with a contented sigh.

"Micah and Daniel could hardly believe their eyes the first night we saw them," Meg said. She didn't add that the tiny insects with their glowing bodies had delighted and mystified her, too. There were no fireflies in the West. Maybe it was too dry or the altitude was too high or something. The boys had a jar full of them on their bedside table. Every morning Micah released them, then he and Daniel caught a new batch in the evening.

"Pots of hanging ferns and pink fuchsias, and old-fashioned wicker furniture, don't you think, Kenneth? With thick chintz-covered cushions." Her mother was talking about porch furniture. "What do you think would be best—to have the furniture painted white or left natural?"

"Umm?" Her dad wasn't on the same wavelength, it was obvious. He glanced over at Meg and gave her a wink. "Sorry, I was thinking about the lower level of the barn. Nothing major, but we need to have a good warm place for them in the winter, don't we?"

"For who?" Meg was puzzled.

"Why, for the stock, of course," Dad answered. "This is a farm, isn't it? I thought we'd see about getting a few hundred head of cattle, maybe some chickens and pigs."

"Oh, Dad!" Meg laughed.

"Well, seriously, I was thinking of a few sheep. Remember how pretty they looked in the fields back in Colorado?"

Colorado! There was no rush of prickly tears, no quick burst of rage when she heard the name now. In fact, she realized with a guilty start, she had hardly given her friends and her old house a thought in the last few days. "I guess I've just been too busy with other things," she told herself. She felt guilty, though, to have so totally abandoned Alicia and the others.

As she sat there on the porch, she tried to put herself back at the house in Littleton. If she were there right now, what would she be doing? Dad wouldn't be home from the office yet, probably. They would have had an early supper without him, and Mom would have read the boys a story and gotten them bathed and tucked into their beds. Meg herself would have been down the street at Alicia's house, playing video games or watching a rented movie. There was never a time when they just sat together like this. There was never this feeling of closeness or, even though it sounded corny, togetherness in their family before. Meg imagined that she could feel contentment in the very air. It enveloped them all.

It was very nearly dark now. In the clear, deep blue of the sky, stars glowed with surprising brilliance. Near the horizon, over the distant trees, the sky was still pale with the waning light of this perfect day. Bats swooped over the lawn, catching insects, and in the distance a dove called before settling down for the night. From behind them, comforting yellow light glowed through the tall windows of the house.

"I do miss Colorado a lot. I guess I'll always miss my friends, and the mountains and everything." Meg paused for a moment, and then spoke again, slowly, as if the thought was just now occurring to her. "But I think I can learn to like it here a lot more than I ever thought I could. This place is beautiful, too, just in a different way. And I think I'm learning to like living in the country."

"We know that it's hard to make adjustments in living, especially something as different as this move was, but we felt very strongly that we needed to simplify our lives. We were all getting too caught up in the rat race. I was working later and later every night, and it seemed like we were spending all our time together running from one store to another. Here the pace can be slower. I can spend more time with all of you here at home." Her father reached over and took her mother's hand. "And we can begin to find out what the really important things are in life," he said softly. "There's one thing I know, Meg. You can't find them in a shopping mall. We weren't finding them in the hectic pace of Denver."

It wasn't the first time she had heard her dad talk like this. Usually Meg would roll her eyes heavenward and say to herself, "There goes Dad on another one of his 'back to the basics lectures.'" But now, for the first time, Meg was really listening. And suddenly it all started to make sense. She was beginning to understand what Dad was talking about. She *felt* what he meant. Even though she had fought it at first, she felt the difference in their family, the closeness. Her dad was more relaxed, and was at home more. Mom sang around the house, and now that Meg really thought about it, Nicholas wasn't as fussy as he had been a few months ago. Maybe her baby brother had felt the difference long before she had.

Simplify our lives, Dad had said. Could it really matter so much? Maybe it did, Meg decided. Maybe this feeling she had right now, this feeling of peace, and closeness with her parents, was one of the important things in life Dad was talking about.

The three of them sat on, now in the dark, in companionable silence. Across the still, cool night air came the whirring sounds of untold numbers of insects. Meg settled more comfortably in her chair, and realized she didn't have that ugly knot inside her anymore, and it felt good—so very good—not to have it there.

— *Eight* —

DEW had soaked her tennis shoes by the time she got back to the house. It was the first time she could ever remember getting up earlier than everyone else in the family. The morning air was cool—the sun was just beginning to peek over the tops of the trees.

By now her parents must be up. She smelled the rich, brown coffee smell before she reached the kitchen door. Dad came in as she put the bouquet of Queen Anne's lace and oxeye daisies in a glass full of water.

"Hey, Punkin," he said when he saw her, "where have you been off to already this morning?"

"I walked out behind the barn and through the orchard. I didn't even know we had an orchard, Dad. I saw lots of apples, and there are peach trees, too. The peaches are tiny and fuzzy."

Mom came into the kitchen with Nicholas on one hip. "You're up with the chickens this morning, Meg," she said with surprise.

"Meg's been out surveying the orchard of the Hamilton

Sheep Farm," Dad told her from behind a box of Cheerios.

"I can just picture sheep grazing under those apple trees," Mom said. "But who, may I ask, will do all the work? Like feeding and shearing? And what will we do with all the wool?"

"Mim told me about a plant that grows in our woods that you can make a yellow dye from," Meg said eagerly. "It's very rare now, but the early pioneers used it for all sorts of medicines. There's pokeweed, and mullein, too; the Indians used them to make dyes. I can show you where they grow."

"I had no idea you knew anything about the plants around here. That's terrific!" Mom sounded very impressed.

"Oh, well. Mim's taught me a little, but there's so much to learn! She knows all about how to use the plants and tells the neatest stories about them. I'm going to start a collection of wildflowers—not the rare ones, but common ones. I thought maybe we could let all the rare flowers grow on our land, to protect them."

"There you go," Dad said with a grin, "you can be the native plant expert at the Hamilton Sheep Farm." But he sounded impressed, too.

It was nice in the big square kitchen. Sunlight streamed in through the east-facing windows. Nicholas banged a spoon against the tray of his high chair while Mom cooked his oatmeal. Dad handed Meg the box of cereal.

"Say, Carin," he said to his wife, "I forgot to mention it last night, but were you up in the attic yesterday?" Her father's words froze Meg as she poured a glass of juice.

"No, I wasn't. Why?"

"That's odd. I noticed the window on the side of the

house facing the drive was open when I came home yesterday afternoon."

Meg had to say something. "I was up there yesterday, Dad. I guess I forgot to shut it." She set the pitcher of juice down. "I'll run up and do it right now."

She had already started out the door when her father called out "Whoa there!" She stopped and turned around.

"I already shut it, Meg. Did you find anything interesting up there?"

"Not really," she answered in a small voice that she hoped sounded normal. She didn't want to lie, and she would tell them eventually, but for right now she couldn't share the chest with anyone else.

Her father shook his head. "It's going to be a big job to get that attic set to rights. I never saw so much old junk in my life."

At that moment Micah and Daniel came into the kitchen, sounding more like a small herd of elephants stampeding than just two small boys, and in the confusion that followed their arrival, the subject of the attic was forgotten. Meg slumped against her chair with relief.

She hurried through her chores that morning as fast as she could. She had to get over to Talley's house. Mim would be wide awake and Meg hoped she could tell her something about the chest in the attic. It was just barely ten o'clock when she finished sweeping the front porch and walk. It was the last thing on the list her mother had given her that morning after breakfast.

Meg put the broom away in the pantry and called out to her mother, who was hanging paintings in the front parlor.

"I'm going over to the log cabin, Mom."

Mrs. Hamilton came down the hall with a hammer in her hand. "To see Talley, Meg?"

"Yes."

Her mother stopped and considered a moment. "I thought you didn't like him. You certainly didn't act like you wanted to go there for tea."

"Well, I didn't at first, but it's okay now. Actually, I want to go visit his great-grandmother. She's so old, and her family's been here for such a long time. I thought she would be interesting to talk to."

"Your dad has met Talley's mother, and from your description of the house, and of Talley's great-grandmother, I think I would love to meet them, too." Mrs. Hamilton looked thoughtful. "Remember how we almost lost the chance to buy this house?"

"Wasn't there another buyer who tried to say that he had gotten his bid in first?" Meg asked.

"That's right. The other buyer is a tough businessman from Cincinnati, and now he's trying to get the Gradeys' property. Jonathan Biggs is his name. He wants to buy all the land around here to build a big housing development. He missed getting our farm, but now he's trying to get the Gradeys' land. He doesn't want the house, just the land. He plans to tear the house down to build a development called Lebanon Hills Estates."

"How could he do that?" Meg cried. "It's not even for sale, is it?"

"No, but Jonathan Biggs claims the house and land never belonged to the Gradey family at all. I don't know any of the details, but apparently it all goes back to the

1800s, when the property was first sold. Your dad says Jonathan Biggs is a big name in real estate, very smart, and always looking for ways to make huge deals and millions of dollars. I got the feeling he might not always be quite honest in his dealings." Her mother sighed, and Meg thought she looked worried. "Anyway, I thought you ought to know about the trouble. Mrs. Gradey went to see your father yesterday. She hopes he'll be able to help her prove that they do own the place. If the Gradeys can't find any proof, there's a chance they could lose it, Dad says. It seems that this Jonathan Biggs character always manages to get his way."

Meg suddenly felt just awful. It seemed so impossible! That house had been in Talley's family practically forever. Mim had been born there! They all belonged there! Maybe that was why Talley's mother looked so tired and worried. Meg wondered if Talley knew.

"Mom, Jonathan Biggs was the man who almost got this house, right?"

"Yes. We were lucky the house came on the market the day we were in the realtor's office in Lebanon, or we never would have gotten it. Even so, Jonathan Biggs put a lot of pressure on us to let him have it. It was a good thing your father's a lawyer, and didn't let Biggs push him out. The man was ruthless, and enraged when he couldn't buy this property out from under us."

Meg thought of Talley's wonderful house, torn down, and fancy new houses, all looking the same, sprinkled close together over the fields. And what about the trees? Jonathan Biggs would be the kind of person who'd bulldoze them all down and cart them off to make room for Lebanon Hills

Estates. It would look just like one of the dozens of housing developments in Denver. Once, she wanted to live in one of them; now the thought of one next door made her stomach drop. Then she thought of something.

"Mom," she said hopefully, "Jonathan Biggs doesn't always win. He didn't get this house. Maybe he won't get Talley's, either."

Daniel and Micah started yelling from the front lawn and her mother turned to go settle the dispute. "I really hope you're right, Meg," she told her over her shoulder. "Be home for lunch, sweetie." Her tone was light, but she looked and sounded worried.

The day would not be as clear as yesterday had been, but the sky was at least a pale blue. Later it would probably be very hot. The dew had already dried from the grass. She followed the path around the barn and the beds of black peppermint, through the pasture, and jumped over the Little Peavine. The Big Oak stood there like an old friend, and she patted its trunk before she turned down the trail through the woods to the log-and-stone house.

Meg saw Mim as soon as she came out of the woods. The old woman was sitting in a rocking chair on the narrow front porch of the log cabin, and she had a pale yellow sweater on over her black dress. She looked as if she'd been there on that porch forever—she seemed to belong to it as much as the slates on the roof or the walls did. The color of her sweater made her skin look as brown and shriveled as the dead leaves that littered the ground in the woods.

Meg tried to put aside the awful sick feeling in her stomach. She was upset about Jonathan Biggs. She was nervous about talking to anyone as old as Mim, but she had to do it. What if Talley wasn't there, and she had to talk to Mim alone? But she didn't know what else to do, where else to begin, and she had to learn what she could about the chest in the attic.

She tried to remind herself that the tea party had been fine after a while, but then she thought again about what Jonathan Biggs planned to do, and she felt even worse.

Meg stopped at the big flat piece of stone that was the front step to the porch. She didn't know what to call Talley's great-grandmother. At tea she had been able to avoid calling the old lady anything. She certainly couldn't call her Mim.

The old woman's dark, bright eyes stared at her, and finally Meg swallowed and said, rather faintly, "Hello." It was all she could think of.

The withered brown leaf of a face broke into a thousand more wrinkles as she smiled the wide grin that was exactly like Talley's.

"Well, well," she said in her soft, creaky voice. "It's that girl with the pretty green eyes." Meg felt herself blush.

"And how are you this morning, Meg Hamilton? How are all those brothers of yours?"

"We're all fine, thank you. How are you?" Meg automatically remembered her manners, but inside she was thinking, "My gosh, there's nothing wrong with her eyesight, or her hearing, or her memory!"

"Well, I expect I'm doing pretty well for such an *old* lady," Mim told her with a gentle chuckle. Meg felt herself blush at the emphasis Mim placed on the word. "I don't believe Talley is to home at the moment. I believe he took his bicycle into town. He usually spends the mornings at the library in the summertime, you know." Mim rocked slightly in her green painted rocker.

Meg cleared her throat nervously. She had hoped Talley could have been there. She hated to be alone with the little old lady. "W-well, I really came here to see you, ah, Mrs.—?" Meg floundered around for something to call the old woman.

"Why don't you call me Mim?" She gave Meg a humorous look. "That's what pretty near everybody in this township calls me. It don't matter that we're not related."

"That'd be great." Meg found herself smiling with relief. It was much easier than she had expected.

"Set yourself down," Mim said, and waved a tiny, age-spotted hand toward the rocker next to her. "I'm glad you came to have a little chat." She shook her head from side to side. "It's surely been a long long time since any young ones lived over in the Rodgers house."

"That's what I wanted to ask you about," Meg said, relieved that the subject of the house had been brought up so quickly. "Who built our house, and who lived in it? And when was it built?" The words came out in a rush. She couldn't come right out and ask if Mim knew anything about an old chest up in the Rodgers attic. She had to see what she could find out without giving the whole thing away.

Mim leaned back in her rocker, and was silent for so long that Meg was afraid she was deaf after all. And then she was worried that Mim had fallen asleep.

"Oh, gosh, why did I even come here? She's so old,

she probably can't even remember who built the house. This was really a stupid idea," she told herself.

It seemed like the silence lasted forever, but it was actually only half a minute or so. Mim's voice rasped over the words, as if she had not spoken them in a long time.

"Who built your house across the creek? Why, the same person who built this log house built it. That would be Tom Rodgers. He sold this little cabin to my grandfather, Jedediah Talmadge, back in 1835, and that same year he moved across the creek into his new white clapboard house. Your house, now." Mim's voice became stern. "Some people claim that never happened, but it's true." She rocked a little harder in her chair. "Some people claim we don't rightly own this house at all."

"Oh, no!" thought Meg, horrified. "I didn't mean to remind her of all their troubles." She sat there in agony, as Mim rocked and talked on.

"That same year my grandfather built on the stone half of this place. 1835. A long time ago now, but my grandfather was a young man then, just startin' out. Jedediah Talmadge. That's who young Talley was named for, o' course. I wish I could call Jedediah Talmadge up from the grave and talk to him for five minutes right now!" Mim said fiercely. "It would save us a whole lot of worry and heartache, I do not doubt." Her black eyes flashed fire.

Then Mim got very quiet, and just sat there staring into space, seeing things that Meg couldn't begin to imagine. Meg clenched her hands together nervously in her lap. The silence seemed to go on forever, when suddenly Mim spoke again.

" 'Course, I never knew Tom Rodgers nor his wife Sarry, but their granddaughter an' I was great friends. That was Miss Rachel Rodgers. I was just a girl like you, and she was an old woman, but not as old as I am now. Almost every day I'd find me some excuse or t'other to go a visitin' at Miss Rachel's. We had some fine times."

Meg found herself leaning forward to hear every soft word. Mim was thinking of happier things now, and Meg was glad. "What sort of things did you do?"

"Oh, goodness, let me see. Well, Miss Rachel had a big old wood stove in her kitchen, and we'd pop corn or make molasses taffy on it in the wintertime." Meg nodded her head. She knew where that stove must have sat, because there was a plastered-over hole in their kitchen wall that must have been for the stovepipe. Her parents had talked about putting in a new wood stove there someday, to make the kitchen warm and cozy in the winter.

"In the summertimes," Mim's voice slipped softly on, "we'd go berryin' an' cook up jam. Or I'd help her slice apples to dry until I thought my arms would fall off. My mama always said I'd rather work for Miss Rachel for free than for anybody else for pay. I guess it was true. I got through my chores lickety-split at home so's I could run across the creek. Miss Rachel loved to have young people around. She always said it made her feel young to have the young folks visit.

"Miss Rachel just seemed to have a knack about her. Yessir, I think it was a knack of bein' alive or lively. And, oh, could she tell stories. She would chatter away, and pretty soon whatever chore we was a'workin' on would be finished."

"What sort of stories did Miss Rachel tell? Fairy tales?" Meg asked, so interested that she was perfectly at ease.

"Goodness, no. Not fairy tales, child. She told us stories from her childhood, real happenings, and about the way life was for her and for her parents before her. I guess you could say Miss Rachel forgot more about this country than most people nowadays know.

"She loved to tell about the ordinary everyday things that happened all those years ago, when she was young. She remembered how the Shakers would drive up from Kentucky to sell baskets and packets of seeds. It was almost a holiday when they came, for everyone would stop their chores to look at goods in the wagon.

"In early summer the menfolk would make the long trip to the Ohio River, down at Cincinnati, with a wagon full of barrels, and sacks of salt. They'd be gone 'most a week, and when they returned, they'd have those barrels packed tight with salted fish to eat in the winter.

"People worked together in those days. If a barn needed to be built or a crop needed to be brought in, why, all a man had to do was ask, he knew he'd have the help of his neighbors. He could depend on't. Things are not the same these days." Mim rocked thoughtfully for a few moments.

"Then, of course, sometimes Miss Rachel would start a-talkin' 'bout big things that happened. Like the war that tore this whole country apart." Mim was quiet, remembering.

Meg hated to sound stupid, but she had to ask. "Which war, Mim?" Why hadn't she ever paid much attention in social studies?

"The Civil War, that was. Miss Rachel was a young

woman when it started, and she was engaged to be married to William Stone. She used to say he was the handsomest boy between here and Pittsburgh. But William went away to the war, and he never came home. He wrote to her regular, and she to him, and one day the letters just stopped. They never found him, just called him 'missing in action.' Lost Will, she always called him after that. I can hear her yet, a-tellin' me 'bout her Lost Will. She never forgot him, and she never married. Too many boys got lost in that war. Too many."

Meg was thoroughly entranced. Here she was, talking to someone who had known a person who actually lived through the Civil War! She felt as if she were in a time machine. The past lay thick all around them. It was cool on the shaded porch, the sunlight coming in green through the leaves of the rosebush that covered the front of the house. It was wonderful to listen to Mim—how could Meg have ever dreaded this?

Mim stopped rocking, and looked off into the distance. She seemed to want to leave the sadness behind. "Oh, and we'd have the finest dances and parties over to Miss Rachel's," she started off in a cheerful voice. "We'd roll up the carpet in the front parlor and the dining room. She had bought a Victrola, an' we had to take turns winding it up. All her nieces and nephews, from Columbus, would come in the summer to stay a week or two."

Meg could have listened for hours to such stories. But it wasn't helping her much with what she had come to track down. The Rodgers house, their house now, was too new to have been the place where the sampler or the chest had been made. And Mim hadn't mentioned anyone named

Sarah Randall, the girl who had made the sampler. Who was she and how did she fit into everything? Meg had to go back even further in time to find the people she was looking for.

"Mim, do you know where Tom Rodgers came from? And when he came here? Do you know?"

"Well, child, let me see. I do know he built this log house in the fall of 1800. That was before Ohio became a state. This is one of the oldest places in these parts still standing. Miss Rachel was Tom's youngest granddaughter, and they left the farm to her, just a young woman, when they died. That all happened long before I was even born. I don't know but that Tom and Sarry might have come from Pennsylvania. They came here from someplace in the east, though, that's certain. That's where all the folks came from that settled this country."

Tom and Sarry Rodgers had built this cabin, Mim said. Sarry?

"Mim!" she interrupted excitedly, "was Tom's wife's name *Sarah*?"

"Yes, she was Sarry Rodgers. That's what folks always called her, but her given name was really Sarah," Mim answered.

At last she had something! Here was a Sarah. Could she have made the sampler?

She crossed her fingers in her lap. "Do you know what Sarah Rodgers's name was before she got married?"

Mim's forehead puckered even more as she gave this question some thought. "Her maiden name? No, I don't recollect that. Don't know as I ever heard that mentioned."

Meg felt as though someone had punched her in the

stomach. Now what could she do to find out if this was the Sarah who had made the sampler? It must be the one, but she wanted to be sure, had to be sure. She had a feeling that if she could find Sarah Randall, she could find out all the secrets of the chest up in her attic. A strange feeling swept over her—suddenly she was overwhelmed with the certainty that what she was searching for was much more important than who made a little girl's sampler. But what?

Still deep in thought that night, Meg mechanically got ready for bed. The new upstairs bathroom was papered with armies of small black-faced sheep on a blue background. It made her think of their own meadow behind the barn. She gathered her hair into a loose bun on top of her head and drew the water in the tub. She peeled off her T-shirt and shorts and left them in a heap on the tile floor.

All the while she was thinking of the things Mim had told her. Dad talked about Ohio as being a settled land, and it had been for well over 175 years, but in the times Mim had spoken of, it was still wild and harsh.

It had been a land covered with thick forests full of danger. There were all the obvious things like panthers and rattlesnakes and Indians, but as Meg thought about it, those dangers were only the beginning.

All kinds of accidents could happen, and there were no hospitals or doctors to set broken bones or stitch up cuts, no veterinarians to care for sick horses or oxen. If food ran low or hunting was poor, there were no stores, of course. It was impossible to imagine how utterly alone Tom and Sarah Rodgers must have been as they traveled through the endless forests to reach the western edge of Ohio. It was all so different from life today that it was hard to even imagine it, but listening to Mim tell about it made it all come alive.

The bathwater was just the right level now, and Meg turned the faucets off with her foot. Mom had let her use a bar of her lavender soap, and its spicy scent enveloped her as she lathered her arms and middle.

"The pioneers of 1800, people like Tom and Sarah, must have been far braver than people today," she decided. "We don't have to face any of the terrible things that they did."

With her back against the cool porcelain of the tub, she let her arms float beside her in the water. She sat up suddenly. "Wait a minute—in a way, we're pioneers, too," she realized. "Of course, we used a station wagon, and not a covered wagon, and stayed in motels and ate at restaurants. But in lots of ways, we are like pioneers.

"We left our home, and came here to Ohio, to a new place, and we have to adjust, just like Tom and Sarah, to a new way of life. And we have to face problems that people two hundred years ago never dreamed would exist. Awful stuff like pollution and nuclear weapons, a soaring crime rate and drugs."

The water trickled through her fingers as she rinsed off. Yeah, the Hamiltons are pioneers. She smiled to herself. "I'll have to tell Mom and Dad that. I think they'll like the idea, too."

—Nine—

"WELL, I suppose that if you want to find out more about the history of Lebanon, the best person to see would be Professor Greene at the historical society." Talley pushed his glasses up on his nose and threw another piece of the stick he was holding into the creek.

Meg leaned back against the root of the Big Oak. It was the hottest part of the day, but under the canopy of the oak's leaves it was almost cool. Callahan trotted purposefully through the underbrush, head down, along the trail of rabbits or a groundhog.

Some small unseen animal rustled through the bushes behind them. At steady intervals a bird trilled a long, complicated song.

"I wonder what kind of bird that is?" Meg asked.

"A house wren, *Troglodytes aedon*, in Latin," Talley promptly replied. "He's in the dogwood tree across the creek. See? That little brownish bird."

"Is there anything you don't know?" she demanded. He grinned at her and shoved his sliding glasses back up on the bridge of his nose. "Of course. Nobody can know everything. I don't know about quantum mechanics yet, but someday when I can study physics, I will."

Meg had never heard of quantum mechanics, and she wasn't even sure she knew what physics was, so she quickly changed the subject.

"This man you know is a professor?"

"Yes, but actually he's retired now. He was the head of the Ancient History Department at Ohio State. One of his hobbies has always been the early history of southwestern Ohio, and right now I know he's doing lots of research on it. He knows more about the early days of Warren County than anybody else around."

Meg had never doubted that Talley could help her figure out what to do next. Now she asked, "Where's the historical society?"

"The Warren County Historical Society. It's at the county seat, which happens to be Lebanon."

"Have you ever gone there? Can anybody just go in? Is it like a museum or something?"

"Yes, yes, and sort of." Talley grinned at her again. He was smart, and kind of a bookworm type, but he had a sense of humor. He could really be funny. "It's more like a library, actually. They do have some displays of old things in glass cases. Pottery and early tools and stuff. And there's a room with furniture and some nineteenth-century textiles."

"Textiles?" Meg sat up. Nineteenth century. "That's the 1800s, isn't it?"

"Mmm," Talley assented absently. He was intently watching an ant carry a large beetle through the leaf mold.

"Too late," Meg muttered under her breath. The sampler had been made in the eighteenth century.

"What?" Talley looked at her. "What do you mean too late?"

"Oh, nothing." She didn't want to tell him too much, at least not yet. "So when can we go there? To the historical society?"

"Let's go tomorrow morning. It closes at three, so we wouldn't have time to ride our bikes all the way in this afternoon. You know, there is someplace I could show you this afternoon that is much closer. And you should be very interested in it."

"Where's that?"

"Did you know that there's an old cemetery up on the hill on the other side of these woods?"

"A real cemetery? Just up on a hill in the middle of nowhere?" Meg had only seen cemeteries by churches in towns, or in big city memorial parks.

"Sure. The Old Rodgers Burying Ground. It was used by the people who lived out here. In the old days, of course, most farmers had their own burying ground." Talley stood up. "It's kind of a steep climb, but the old road is still there. Come on."

Meg felt her heart thump with excitement as she got to her feet and followed Talley through the trees. "Are there tombstones?"

"Oh yes. There's even a little stone wall around the place, and a hundred years or so back someone planted cedar trees and rosebushes around it. It's pretty overgrown, of course, but the headstones are still legible."

It felt eerie to be headed for a cemetery through the

thick woods. All of a sudden everything seemed spooky—even Callahan thrashing through the underbrush sounded sinister to Meg.

She shivered. Would she find full names and dates on these stones? Would she find Sarah Randall?

As they walked the ground rose slightly. On the right now the trees thinned and Meg could see fields full of corn. "That's Mr. Ryan's corn, but it's your field. Mr. Ryan rents the land but it's part of the old Rodgers place," Talley said.

"All that's ours?"

"The land the burying ground is on is part of your farm, too."

"Oh," Meg said weakly. She'd had no idea. "I guess I was too busy protesting everything about our new home to find out much about it," she said to herself.

They walked along the edge of the cornfield for a short distance, then Talley veered to the left up a narrow dirt track. It could not be called a road, Meg decided. Weeds choked in on either side and grew in abandon down the center.

"It's been a long time since a wagon has come up this way," Talley called over his shoulder. "About two years ago some of the people around here had a cleanup day at the burying ground, and Mr. Ryan drove Mim up in his truck."

Both of them were a little out of breath with the climb. The hill rose quickly and was heavily wooded.

At the top of the hill, the wagon track curved. They made the turn, and right in front of them was the Old Rodgers Burying Ground.

"It's so tiny," Meg said with surprise.

"Most private burying grounds are small," Talley replied. "Sometimes there are only two or three graves. This one has eight."

The track took them through an opening in the dry stone wall. The ground was thick with fallen leaves. Dark green ivy trailed along the wall and in places climbed high up into trees. At other spots wild rosebushes tumbled over the wall in huge mounds. Tall cedar trees stood guard in a row along one side.

"You almost always see cedar trees planted around old cemeteries. They were kind of symbolic of eternal life, since they're always green. And they look dignified and somber, I think." Talley's voice sounded loud in the stillness of the place.

He led her first to three little white headstones that were almost buried under leaves. They had to scoop armfuls aside before they could read the inscriptions. Lambs had been carved on the top of each marker. Green moss had grown in the crevices, so the writing was easy to read.

"Laura Clark, daughter of William and Rebecca Clark. Died May 14, 1858, aged three years, two months, eight days," Meg read the first one.

Talley read the next stone. "Anna Clark, died May 16, 1858, aged four years, ten months, four days."

Meg moved to the last little stone. "Margaret Clark, died May 17, 1858, aged six years, five months, nineteen days. Oh, Talley, I wonder what they died from?"

"Measles. The Clarks had the farm where Mr. Ryan lives. They lost all their children in four days."

"I didn't know people could die from just measles."

"Whole families often died from measles in the 1800s.

They'd often develop pneumonia, and there were no antibiotics then, no vaccines."

Meg read the names again. "Poor children," she said softly. "And poor parents. It must have been so hard for them."

"Come look over here," Talley called from the far corner of the burying ground.

The stones Talley pointed to leaned crookedly. "These are my great- great- great- great-grandparents. In other words, my fourth great-grandparents."

"Jedediah Talmadge," Meg read. "Hester, Consort of Jedediah Talmadge." At Meg's questioning glance, Talley explained.

"It means wife of—the term is obsolete now, of course."

"Of course," murmured Meg.

"I did have to look it up, you know," Talley said with a grin. "Come over here. You know these people."

"I do?"

She followed him to the next group of stones.

"Rachel Rodgers. Miss Rachel! I *do* feel as if I know her," Meg said softly. After a moment she moved with Talley to the next stone.

"Christian and Mary Rodgers. They were Miss Rachel's parents," Talley said.

The last stones were hard to read. Meg bent close to them. "Thomas Rodgers." She looked up at Talley. "This was the man who built your cabin?"

"Yes. And your house, too. Look at this next one. It has another obsolete term."

"Sarah, relict of Thomas Rodgers." Was this the Sarah who made the sampler?

"Relict means she was widowed," Talley continued with a grimace. "The dictionary says that word is archaic, and I'm sure glad. It makes the poor lady sound as if she was a leftover." If Talley noticed that Meg seemed lost in thought he made no comment.

"Talley, there aren't dates on Sarah's stone."

"They've worn away. Feel right here. Those slight indentations were the dates. You can't see Tom's, either. They were the first people buried up here, and the stone used for their markers seems to be softer. It has worn away quicker than the other stones."

Meg was thoughtful as they walked back down the narrow road. Those people buried up there on the hill had been there so long that their names were almost gone, and yet they had lived right where Meg's family lived now. They must have had that beautiful chest, and known all about the things that were in it, yet it was all a mystery to Meg. Maybe Talley's professor could help.

She watched Talley walking next to her. She liked him a lot, but not at all as she imagined she would like other boys someday. Talley was a friend, but not a boyfriend. She had never thought about being good friends with a boy, but with Talley she could be.

He was quiet, too. Meg saw that he looked lost in thought, worried, and she knew why.

"Talley—I know about the trouble your family's having with that awful Jonathan Biggs," she blurted out. "I know that my dad can help you. He's a good lawyer."

"I know," he said after a moment, his voice tight with emotion. "I'm glad you know. I wondered if you did."

There didn't seem to be anything else to say. Once

she thought she saw him wipe his eyes, as if there were tears there. She felt so badly for him. She remembered how awful she had felt about leaving her home in Littleton. Somehow, it must be even worse for Talley. His family was being cheated, and his home would be torn down. Meg looked around her at the quiet woods. All this would be gone. She felt like crying herself.

They returned to the Big Oak in silence. "I'll see you in the morning," Talley told her. "I need to get home now."

Home—for how much longer? Her father would come up with something to stop Jonathan Biggs, he just had to.

She watched Talley disappear down the path, then turned to whistle for Callahan. He came galloping up from the creek, two-thirds wet and huge paws muddy. It looked as if he had explored every inch of the Little Peavine. Pieces of grass and fern hung from his mouth. He sat obediently at Meg's feet, gazing up at her with his wise brown eyes. Impulsively, Meg bent and hugged him, paying no heed to the wet fur.

"Oh, Cal! There just has to be something that we can do! We can't just stand by and watch them lose their home!" The big dog whined, responding to the unhappiness in her voice. She stood and brushed off the front of her T-shirt. "But what can we do against Jonathan Biggs?" she whispered to herself.

They had arranged to meet in front of the Hamiltons' house at eight thirty the next morning. Meg had made two peanut butter sandwiches and fixed a plastic bottle with apple juice the night before. She put it in the freezer, and in the morning when she took it out, it was frozen solid. By lunchtime, it would be thawed, but still cold and just right to drink.

Her blue day-pack still smelled faintly of wood smoke from the last time she had used it on a trip to the mountains, and she had to shake out a few pine needles before she put in her lunch, but she hardly gave it a thought. Colorado seemed very far away, but that was all right. She didn't stop to think that pine needles and pinyon smoke would have brought tears only a week ago. She didn't have time to think about anything but today.

Last night, before she went to bed, she remembered a book she once read about a knight who had gone on a quest to find something of great worth. She liked to think that she was going on a quest, too. A quest, or a treasure hunt. She wasn't expecting to find anything of great worth, like that knight. If she could find out who made the things in the chest she would be satisfied. She doubted that the things up there in the attic had much monetary worth. They smelled so bad, for one thing, and they were all pretty brown and faded. But those old pieces of cloth and that wooden chest were rich with memories and should never have been forgotten, she was sure of it. She wanted to find those memories again.

She heard Talley clatter up the road before he actually came into view, and she got her bike and started down the drive to meet him.

Talley had a brown paper sack in his wire basket, and two books. "I thought that since we'd be right there, I'd stop by the library and return these two."

This was a safe subject. "Did you read them overnight?" Meg knew he had only gotten them the day before.

Talley looked embarrassed. "Mmm." He pretended to rearrange the lunch in his basket.

She watched him for a second as he started off on that dilapidated bike of his. Then she jumped on her bike and stepped down hard on the pedals to catch up.

—Ten—

THEY locked up their bikes around the wrought iron railing of the historical society building. Meg was worried that they'd get in trouble for doing that, but Talley was unperturbed. "No problem. I do it all the time. Nobody minds."

It was just after nine thirty, when the place was supposed to open. On their way up the steps, Meg looked at the building. It was red brick, three stories tall but kind of narrow. The brick looked old, all faded and soft. Trim around the windows was painted white, and the shutters were black. The front door was a shiny dark green, and there was a brightly polished brass plaque mounted on it that said THE WARREN COUNTY HISTORICAL SOCIETY— LEBANON, OHIO. It was a very impressive-looking place. Red geraniums and white petunias were planted in half barrels on the wide sidewalk, and everything was dappled in the shade of the huge old sycamores that lined South Street.

Talley turned the doorknob, and the heavy door swung open without a sound. Inside it seemed dark at first, but as

Meg's eyes grew accustomed to the changed light she began to pick out details of the interior.

They stood in a wide hall. A stairway rose on the left, its steps covered with a deep red carpet. Along the walls of this hall were glass-fronted display cabinets, just like the ones Talley had described. Looking quickly, she saw lots of brown- and tan-colored pottery, and all sorts of small tools and nails. There was a narrow pair of long, once-white gloves, and a lady's fan made out of ivory and feathers. In another case were several old guns and pistols, some rusty-looking cannonballs, and a tarnished sword. Nothing to get excited about, she decided.

"Where's this Professor Greene?" she whispered to Talley. She hadn't seen any signs saying NO TALKING or QUIET PLEASE, but this seemed to be a place that you just naturally whispered in.

"The professor has an office upstairs," Talley whispered back, "but let's check the rooms down here, first." He led the way into the room on the left. This looked exactly like a library. There were shelves all along the walls full of dusty volumes, and a fireplace with two comfortable-looking chairs. A woman was leafing through a thick book at one of the four worktables in the center of the room. She was the only person in the room, and she looked up at them and smiled briefly, then continued with her book.

The room on the opposite side of the hall was full of tables loaded with strange equipment. Meg had no idea what any of it was. She threw Talley a questioning look.

"These are microfilm readers." He pointed to large, boxy-looking things with viewing screens. "People can read documents and old records that have been put on film with one of these. Census records and things like that. You can order a film with the 1860 census for, oh, say Boston, Massachusetts, that's been photographed on a film. Instead of going to Boston and looking through big books of records, you can come to a place like this.

"These smaller machines are called microfiche readers." He went to a filing cabinet and opened a drawer.

He took out a four-by-six-inch rectangle of what looked like the negative of a photograph, or the stuff X rays are taken on. "This is a microfiche." Meg looked blank. "You know what *micro* means. And *fiche* is French for card," he patiently explained. "So literally it means small card. You can photograph hundreds of names on one of these, or pages and pages from a book. Then you use one of these things"—he indicated the machine on the table—"to read it."

"Oh." Meg shook her head slightly, puzzled. "But what's it all for?"

"For doing genealogical research, of course."

"Oh." Still puzzled.

Talley tried again. "For doing family history. Looking up your ancestors. A lot of people do it as a hobby. They try to see how far back they can go, and if they were related to any famous people. My mom does it. She comes here often. That's how I know Professor Greene."

"Oh." The kid was amazing, he really was. Meg looked around the room. "Well, he's not here."

"Let's try his office. He usually works on his book up there in the mornings." Talley started out the door.

Meg followed. Her head was swimming with microfiche and genealogy, and now Talley was going to take her to meet a professor who was writing a book.

Their footsteps were muffled on the thick carpet. When they reached the second floor they could hear music. Talley led the way down a hall toward the sound. He stopped in front of a door that said simply HYRUM B. GREENE. He frowned for a few seconds, listening to the music, and then his round, freckled face split into a grin.

"Another one of his hobbies is baroque music," he whispered. "We have this sort of game. He always asks me what piece of music he's listening to, and he usually stumps me. But today I know what it is!"

He rapped sharply on the door, and almost immediately a deep voice rumbled, "Come in!"

Meg nearly jumped at the sound. Talley threw her a look over his shoulder. "Don't be scared," he told her.

The room they entered was filled with books. Books of all shapes and sizes spilled out of ceiling-high shelves, across tables and chairs. Stacks of them stood in corners. Perched precariously on one low pile of them stood a carved music stand with a violin propped across it. Squeezed in between some of the books were stone sculptures that Meg thought might be Egyptian, and there were several large, ancient-looking pottery jugs lying about in no apparent order. In the middle of all these books and papers and artifacts was Professor Hyrum Greene.

The first thing Meg noticed about the man was his size. He didn't look at all the way she thought a college professor would look. An average-sized man would have been dwarfed by the mountains of books in the room, but

Talley's professor was enormous. He had wide shoulders, and a large head with a mane of curly, graying hair that made him seem even bigger. His skin was the warm dark brown color of coffee. He smiled when he saw Talley, stood up, and pushed his glasses up onto his forehead. He didn't say anything, just stood there smiling with his arms folded across his massive chest, as though he was waiting for something.

All this time the music swelled louder around them in the small room. Meg could hear violins chase each other in a complicated melody that was faintly familiar to her.

Talley waited until the music ended. Then he simply said, "Pachelbel's Canon," and Professor Greene's eyes opened wide in surprise.

"Good for you, Talley. Of course, that's a popular piece, not at all obscure. But well done all the same!" His voice seemed to growl up from deep inside him, and Meg noticed that Talley flushed and grinned even wider with the praise.

Professor Greene reached behind him and turned off the tape player that was just visible behind a heap of books and papers. He looked at Meg. "How do you do?" he asked. The ordinary words rolled off his tongue with a flourish. Meg thought he sounded like an actor, and she felt herself flushing just like Talley.

"This is Meg Hamilton, Professor Greene," Talley introduced her. "Her family just moved into the old Rodgers farm."

"Ah, yes, out on Little Peavine Creek." The professor's huge hand enveloped hers. "It is indeed a pleasure to meet you, Miss Hamilton."

Meg wasn't sure exactly what she replied. There was

something about the professor that made her feel awkward and very young and foolish. Professor Greene walked around the corner of his desk and sat down on the edge of it, unmindful of the scattered papers. He again folded his arms across his broad chest and smiled. "Sit down, both of you," he told them, and indicated the worn blue chairs behind them. "Just put those books on the floor. What can I do for you this morning, Talley? And how is Mim?"

"She's just fine, and wanted to know when you'd be out next to visit. Actually, sir, Meg had some questions she wanted to ask you about the early history of Lebanon."

"I asked Talley to bring me here to meet you, Professor Greene," Meg practically gulped the words out in her hurry. She glanced at Talley, guiltily. She hadn't told him the real reason she wanted to meet the professor. "You see, I need to find out some information about the people who built the house we live in. Tom Rodgers. And Sarah Rodgers." She knew she was talking too fast, but she couldn't help it.

Professor Greene gave her an appraising look. "Interested in the history of your new home, is that it? That's excellent. Admirable, and most unusual in a person your age." He got up and walked back to his chair. "Talley may have told you I have an interest in this area myself." He reached around behind him to a file cabinet, and pulled out a folder. "Ask away," he said. "I just may be able to be of some assistance."

Meg haltingly explained what she needed to know. "So mostly I need to know what Sarah Rodgers's name was before she married, and where she came from," she finished.

The professor was leafing through his file as she spoke,

and as soon as she finished he said, "Ah, yes, I thought I had it," and handed her a piece of paper.

Talley leaned over to get a look at the paper, too. And there it was, right in her hands. The information had been copied from a church record, and it gave Sarah's full name as Sarah Randall Rodgers—born 1776 died 1865—aged eighty-nine years.

That birth date meant that Sarah Randall had been ten years old in 1786. And that was the year she made the sampler. The dates for Sarah Rodgers fit. Meg couldn't hide a smile of excitement. She had found the girl who made the sampler, and it was wonderful to think that that same girl, Sarah Randall, had grown up and married Tom Rodgers and come to Ohio, and had eventually lived in the very house the Hamilton family now lived in. Yesterday Meg had stood at her grave.

But Meg had more questions now. She wanted to know where the sampler was made, and who had worn the baby clothes and that blue coat. "Do you know where Sarah Randall lived when she was a little girl?" she asked.

The professor lifted his glasses up onto his forehead again. "Yes, I believe she and Thomas, her husband, came out to Ohio from western New Jersey in 1800."

"And built the cabin on Little Peavine Creek," Talley added.

"Do you know anything about her family?" Meg was afraid this would be a dead end, and she crossed her fingers in her lap.

There was a long silence while Professor Greene skimmed over the other sheets in the file. "No," he said finally. He closed the folder and stood up. "But our friend here"—he nodded to Talley—"can help you in that area with his knowledge of the records downstairs. Thomas and Sarah were married at a town called Hopewell, which was then in the county of Hunterdon, in 1795." He waited, watching Talley.

Talley was thinking. "I guess the first place to look would be the census records." His forehead wrinkled. "But there isn't too much information that far back. We might have better luck with the county tax lists, and church records." His forehead smoothed out and he smiled. "And we could look in the probate records for wills!"

"That should all keep you busy for this morning, at least," the professor said, "and will let me get back to my manuscript. Happy hunting!" his deep voice rumbled after them.

Downstairs in the library Talley headed straight for the gray metal cabinets marked u.s. census records. "While I look in here for a film that might help us, you check out the books in the New Jersey section over along that wall," he told her, and pointed to the shelves of reference books that lined the walls of the room.

Meg took out the small notebook and pencil she had snatched off the kitchen counter and stuck in her backpack with lunch, and went to work.

Two hours later they stopped to eat. Meg's hands felt grubby from handling what must have been two dozen old books, and her head ached from reading tiny printing on age-darkened pages.

She closed her notebook and followed Talley out into the street without saying a word.

"We can go eat in the park," Talley told her. "Leave the bikes. The park's just around the block, off South Street, and right across from the Warren County Courthouse."

She knew the park. Suddenly it looked familiar to her, and she realized that her father's office was just on the other side from where they had entered. She didn't mention it to Talley, though. In fact Meg was so quiet that Talley gave her a long look, started to say something, then changed his mind and led the way to the small, tree-filled park. At last he did speak.

"You really worked hard in the library. What exactly is it that you're looking for? It's more than just the history of your house, isn't it?"

Meg gave a noncommittal "Um" and didn't meet Talley's glance.

He tried again. "You appeared to be very interested in the Revolutionary War veteran's list from New Jersey." Meg said nothing, but suddenly bent to tie a sneaker that had not been untied.

Talley gave up. "Would you like to sit at a table or on the ground?" he asked when they were standing just inside the South Street entrance to the park.

"A table, I guess. Or the ground would be fine. I don't care." Meg was so involved in her own thoughts she hardly heard what Talley said. She had to tell people now about the chest in her attic. After what she had discovered, it couldn't be just hers anymore. It was too important. Of course, she didn't have actual proof, but she thought she had the whole thing figured out correctly. Why else would the old blue jacket have been saved all those years, with all the other special things? It was more than just a play coat or part of a costume. It had been saved because it was something special, too.

Talley picked a shady spot under a large horse chestnut tree and sat without a word. A couple of little kids were running around the far end of the park. Their mother was sitting at one of the picnic tables, with a book, and a dog on a leash. The end of the park closest to them was deserted.

They sat down on the soft green grass and started to eat. At least Talley ate. Meg sat staring at the wrapper of the peanut butter sandwich in her lap. Talley was on his second sandwich before she looked up and said, "I found something up in the attic of our house that I think must be pretty important."

Talley stopped chewing and stared at her.

"At first I thought I could just keep what I found, that it could be my secret, but now I know I have to tell people about it, and I want you to hear about it first. And then you can tell me who needs to know about it next. Maybe your professor, I don't know." Meg stopped to take a breath, and then told Talley what she had discovered in the attic of the Rodgers farmhouse, and the discovery she had just made in the library.

—Eleven—

FOR several moments Talley just stared at her. She was about ready to ask him what was wrong—hadn't he heard her? But finally he said, "Oh my gosh," very softly. He took off his glasses and rubbed his face with both hands, then slowly put his glasses on again.

Meg was surprised that Talley, who usually was never at a loss for words, seemed to be overwhelmed. His face had gotten very red.

At last he said, "What an incredible discovery, Meg. It's absolutely amazing!" His face was split by the widest grin she had ever seen. She knew that Talley, out of all the people she would have to tell, would probably be the most excited by her find. She thought he would demand to see the chest right away. That's certainly what she would have done. But Talley accepted the existence of the chest. He wanted to find as many facts about its history as possible.

His forehead wrinkled up with thought. "That chest and everything in it must have been up in the attic of the Rodgers place ever since it was built. I don't think Mim knows about it. Anyway, she never mentioned a chest like that as far as I can remember."

"What do we do next?" Meg asked him.

"Let's go ask Mim about it. There's a chance she'll remember hearing something about it if we jog her memory."

They were bent over, picking up sandwich wrappers and stuffing them into their packs, when a voice spoke right behind them.

"Meg! This is a surprise!" They both turned around, and there, with a newspaper under his arm, stood her father. "I thought I'd sit over here for a while on my lunch hour and try to clear away some of the cobwebs." He smiled at Talley. "What have you two been up to this morning?"

"We went to the library," Meg and Talley said at the same time. After all, the historical society did have a library in it. They weren't lying. Meg was relieved that Talley, too, seemed to feel the time was not right to talk about the chest.

"That's terrific." Her father grinned at them. He was big on reading.

A car door slammed behind them on the street, and Talley looked past Mr. Hamilton. "Wow," he said softly. "Will you look at that!"

Meg and her father complied. Parked against the curb of the street was the longest, sleekest limousine Meg had ever seen. It looked ridiculously out of place there next to the seesaws and swings of the children's play area of the park. The windows were tinted so darkly that they couldn't see the occupants of the car, but a uniformed chauffeur opened the back door as they stood there staring.

Meg thought she sensed her father stiffen. "He must recognize the man," she thought. She herself had never seen him before. He was of below average height, but his large head made him look powerful, and somehow menacing. Balding, his sharp, hawklike nose and bushy black eyebrows reminded Meg of a beetle. He wore a pale gray, almost white suit, and carried a very large leather case. With barely a glance to either side, he strode purposefully into the county courthouse across the street.

Her father looked thoughtful, and ran his hand through his hair. "I wonder what he's up to now," he said quietly to himself. He seemed to have forgotten that Meg and Talley were with him.

"Who was that man, Dad? Do you know him?" Meg asked.

"That was Jonathan Biggs, wasn't it?" Talley asked. "My mother described him to me. He's the man who's trying to take our farm."

Talley said it quietly, but Meg knew him well enough by now to know that seeing the man had upset him. He seemed to be tight within himself. She couldn't even imagine how Talley must feel at the prospect of losing his home. She felt sick herself.

"That's right," her father answered. "That man is a whole lot of trouble, and I don't know of one respectable person in this town who would deal with him." Kenneth Hamilton shook his head sadly. "Unfortunately, money is very important, and a lot of money can do amazing things."

Meg was alarmed by her father's defeated tone of voice. "Dad, that man isn't going to be allowed to take Talley's house, is he?"

Her father sighed. "He has a case. He's offered the county a great deal of money to buy the property, and Talley's mother has so far been unable to show proof of ownership. It's a complicated business, kids. It doesn't happen too often here in the Midwest or the East, but it was a fairly common occurrence in the West. Land can descend through a family for generations without anyone ever checking the deed. Sometimes accurate surveys were never made, and people could discover that their house, that had been in the family for seven, eight generations, had been built on a neighbor's piece of property. What it all boils down to is we may not be able to stop Jonathan Biggs."

Talley stood stiff and straight, with his hands clenched at his sides. "My mother and Mim have been through all the old papers and everything. They've searched everywhere, and they can't find any information about the house." His voice was strained. "But I know it must be somewhere."

Kenneth Hamilton put his hand on Talley's shoulder. "I wanted to make sure you knew that we have a tough battle ahead of us, but let's not give up hope yet, Talley. Some of the records are still being searched over there." He nodded toward the courthouse. "There are boxes and boxes of dusty old records, forgotten by everyone, so we aren't beat yet by a long shot."

Talley managed a weak smile, but Meg thought her father did not sound as encouraging as his words seemed.

As she stood there, feeling sick for Talley, her thoughts were drawn, inexplicably it seemed, to the old wooden chest in her attic. Her father's words, "forgotten by everyone," echoed in her head.

*   *   *

Waiting in Talley's living room, Meg traced the outline of the arrowheads with her finger. A dozen of them had been mounted in a circular design and framed in a simple black frame.

She looked up as Talley came through the door. "My grandfather found them all here on our land. He always kept an eye out for Indian relics while he did the spring plowing. Usually that's when they turn up, especially after a good hard rain. Sometimes we still find arrowheads and trade beads." He sighed, and Meg could imagine that he was thinking that there might never be a field plowed on their farm again, only houses and streets and sidewalks.

"Mim says to come in her room. She was just getting up from her nap, but she said she'd love a visit," he told her.

They had ridden straight to Talley's house from Lebanon, and Meg imagined her face was as red and sweaty as Talley's, but that didn't matter.

She followed Talley down a narrow, dark hall to his great-grandmother's room.

Mim was sitting in a small, straight-backed chair by the window. The outward-facing wall of the room was striped, dark brown wood and clean, whitewashed chinking, like all the walls of the cabin, but the interior walls were papered in a soft, delicate design. Meg realized with a start that it was the same wallpaper as her bedroom, and before she even said hello, she cried out, "Mim, you have my wallpaper!"

The tiny woman's face almost disappeared in wrinkles when she smiled. "Oh, I imagined you must have the rose bedroom. Miss Rachel and I papered that room, oh let me see now, it must be close to eighty years ago, and we had enough left over to do this room, too." Her eyes traveled the walls. "It's held up real well I think. When we first did that room, it was for the girls' guest bedroom. Miss Rachel's nieces from Columbus liked to come and stay." Mim's face softened. "They were about my age. Phoebe and Maude and I used to have some gay old times in that rose-papered bedroom. We'd oftentimes stay up until the rooster crowed, laughing and talking, and doing our hair all different outlandish ways." She laughed softly. "My, what times we had!"

Meg listened to her with shining eyes. She tried to picture the rose bedroom, her room, with those girls of over three-quarters of a century ago in it. She had thought it cold and strange, and it almost made her shiver now to think of the "gay times" Mim spoke of. They sounded like the slumber parties she and her old friends back in Littleton had had. Girls eighty years ago had slumber parties, too, that sounded just like the ones girls had today. Suddenly, the rose bedroom didn't seem strange, it felt good, and it felt like it was hers. When school started and she met girls her age, she would have slumber parties and add to the memories already in the room.

Meg glanced around Mim's room. The bed had a tall headboard and footboard, carved with bunches of fruit and grape leaves. The wood was dark and rich-looking, and the whole bed was covered with a crazy quilt made from scraps of velvet and satin in deep jeweled colors. The small room only had space for a dresser and mirror, and on one wall hung a portrait of an old lady with lace at her neck. The paint was dark and cracked with age. Mim noticed Meg staring.

"That was given to me by Miss Rachel. It is her grandmother, Sarry Rodgers, and it was painted in 1860, when she was a very old woman."

Talley, usually so calm, squirmed impatiently next to her. "Mim, did you ever go up in Miss Rachel's attic?"

"Up in Miss Rachel's attic?" Mim repeated, and Meg could understand her puzzlement. "Well, a few times, I expect. Sometimes Miss Rachel hung her muslin bags of dried apples from the rafters in the attic. It was good and dry there, with a good roof over it. Tom Rodgers built a good solid house, my grandpa used to say."

"Did you ever see an old chest in the attic, a wooden chest?" Meg asked. She held her breath.

Mim hesitated only a moment. "The only chest I ever saw in that house was the cherry wood chest that Sarry Rodgers's father built for her mother the year that they got married. That was the chest Miss Rachel called the Keepsake Chest. Yes, she showed it to me once. But it was never up in the attic. Very special it was, and full of old things, old even then, all that time ago." Mim leaned back in her chair and sighed. "I wonder what ever became of that chest."

Meg could hardly hold still with excitement. Mim knew all about it, and even called it by a name, the Keepsake Chest. It was a good name.

The old lady sat straight up again and looked first at Talley, then Meg, with her old dark eyes sharp and bright. "How do you know of that chest?"

"Meg found it, Mim. It's up in the attic of the Rodgers

house!" Talley's face was so flushed that his thousands of freckles seemed to disappear. It was the most excited Meg had ever seen him.

"That attic is full of junk, Mim," Meg explained. "I found it under an old blanket, just left and forgotten."

It was Mim's turn to be surprised. "Is that a fact!" she exclaimed. "That lovely thing, up there all those years! I can't believe the relatives that closed up the house didn't care about it."

"Maybe they didn't know about it," Talley said.

"And all those years the house stood empty." Mim shook her head in disbelief. "What a treasure, just left by the wayside!"

"Meg's already guessed about some of the things in the chest, Mim. Can you remember what Miss Rachel showed you?" Talley asked.

"Why, yes, I can see those things like it was only yesterday that Miss Rachel showed them to me. You children sit down, there on the bed. That's right. It won't hurt that quilt a bit.

"It was in the fall of the year, and oh, my, it must have been about 1908 or thereabouts. I was just about your age, Meg. Miss Rachel and I had been picking the last of the chrysanthemums, and we put them in large crocks that had been her mother's, along with red and yellow leaves from the maples and the brown leaves of the oaks. I remember we needed another crock, to set out on the porch, and Miss Rachel thought that there was one up in the attic. I guess she was in one of her rememberin' moods, because when we had found the crock, she said to me, 'Alice Anne, I would like to show you my most prized possessions.' I always thought that Miss Rachel took a special shine to me, and I think she knew that I would think as highly of her prized possessions, as she called 'em, as she did herself.

"Anyway, she led the way back downstairs to her best bedroom, and pointed to the old wooden chest at the end of the four-poster bed. 'There it is, Alice Anne. The things that are in that chest could tell quite a story if they could talk. That chest is full of memories, because of the things that are in it, and for the places it has been.'

"She perched me on the edge of a chair, and knelt in front of the chest on the turkey red carpet, and never mind that she had her second-best blue serge skirt on."

Mim stopped a moment to rest. Her voice was tired from so much talking. Meg and Talley waited quietly for her to continue. The green trees and hot summer sun outside the window seemed unreal; Mim's story had transported them back over eighty years to a crisp fall day and Miss Rachel's best bedroom.

The lace curtains at the window moved with a slight breeze, and Mim continued, her voice stronger for the rest. " 'This chest,' Miss Rachel told me, 'was made by my great-grandfather. See the year he made it? 1774. That was just before he went to fight the War of Independence.'

"And then Miss Rachel opened up the chest, and the first thing she took out of it was a blue jacket. 'This is his soldier's coat from that war. He didn't get it until near the end of the war, after the French decided to help us and sent supplies. That was right after the bad winter at Valley Forge, in Pennsylvania. All winter long my great-grandpa shivered and shook in the cold with only a thin blanket, and as soon as spring came, he got himself this fine warm coat.' "

Meg and Talley exchanged a look. "Your hunch was right," Talley said. "The Joshua Randall you found on the Revolutionary War index was Sarah's father." He grinned at her. "That was a pretty good piece of detective work." "I hoped he was the right one. Knowing the town he came from helped a lot." Meg turned back to Mim. "Do you remember anything else Miss Rachel showed you?"

"Why of course I do. There were some lovely things in that chest. Quilts and the sweetest little baby clothes that Miss Rachel's ancestors wore. And she showed me a sampler that her grandmother, old Sarry Rodgers, made when she was a girl. I thought about that just the other day, Meg, when you asked me what her maiden name had been. I know it must have been on that sampler, but I couldn't remember it."

"It was Randall, Mim," Talley told her, "and the man who made the chest, Sarah's father, was named Joshua Randall."

"We don't know who his wife was, the one he made the chest for, but we do know her initials. They were carved on the chest. C.P. It said J.R.—C.P. Now we know who J.R. was," Meg said. "I wonder if we'll ever find out who C.P. was?"

"We can try to find her," Talley said. "We'll check marriage records in New Jersey for the year 1774, to see if Joshua Randall is listed. If the wife's initials are C and P . . ."

"We'll know we have the right one!" Meg finished. She gave him a grin.

Mim spoke again. "Meg, have you looked to see what is in the Keepsake Chest? Are any of these things still in it?"

"Oh, Mim, everything is just as you described. It's all there, just the way Miss Rachel must have left it." On impulse Meg reached out and took Mim's hand, and fought back the tears that suddenly pricked her eyes.

Mim had made the past seem so real, not something that only happened in a history book. The things that had been placed in the Keepsake Chest were the treasures of a family, their memories. And yet, after Rachel Rodgers died, it appeared there was no one left to care about the quilts or the sampler. The coat with the wonderful story and the carefully preserved baby clothes were lost to the hands that were meant to have a link to the past through them. Nobody cared, and the Keepsake Chest sat in an empty farmhouse for years and years and was finally sold with an attic full of junk. It was almost too much for Meg to bear.

Mim squeezed her hand. "I know, child. I know just what you're feelin'. It's a darn shame. A darn shame for sure."

— *Twelve* —

JONATHAN BIGGS and his attorney huddled together at the big table in the conference room. They sat staring at the papers in front of them, but Jonathan, at least, didn't really read them. He already knew what they said. He had gone over them carefully several times. A satisfied smile crept over his beetlelike face. He had won, and that pleased him a great deal.

He was going to give the statement by the court to that smart lawyer, Kenneth Hamilton, and it would be sweet to see the look on his face. Maybe Kenneth Hamilton had won the first round, sneaking the Rodgers farm away from him, but this time he had lost. Jonathan Biggs had it in writing, all legal. The Gradey property was his.

Oh, sure, the Gradeys had thirty days to vacate the premises, but that was just a technicality. He had already talked to his heavy-equipment manager, and they planned to start bulldozing, recontouring the land, as soon as the Gradeys left. He rubbed his chin and considered. They might even be able to start before the family moved out.

It was just a technicality, after all. He'd have his lawyers check on it. The county officials were willing to do almost anything he asked of them. In fact, he decided that there would be no reason not to start right away on the earth moving and tree removal. There was no reason to wait for the Gradeys to be out.

The meeting was short and to the point. Mrs. Gradey came through the heavy paneled door, followed by her lawyers. She was quiet and very pale, and did not look at Jonathan Biggs or his attorney.

Kenneth Hamilton shook hands all around, with a slight air of distaste that he tried to hide with politeness. It didn't bother Biggs at all. He never let emotion get in the way of business. If he had, he'd never be where he was today.

This was business, and that was all that mattered. And, anyway, the Gradey woman was illegally occupying that piece of land. Obviously she had no claim to it that could stand up in a court of law. The county was delighted to find that they apparently owned the land, and that Jonathan Biggs wanted to buy it. A big new housing development meant more people in the county, and more people meant more tax money. Yes, the county officials could hardly wait for the deal to be finalized.

Mr. Hamilton received the papers from Jonathan Biggs's attorney with a brief nod of his head. He read them over carefully. The way Biggs played the game, you couldn't be too careful. It would be just like him to try to slip something else into the proceedings.

This was the most frustrating case Kenneth Hamilton had ever handled. Poor Elizabeth Gradey. She had searched everywhere, even helping the law clerks from his office dig through boxes of old documents in the basement of the courthouse, but it was no good. He hated to see a thing like this happen, but it was a matter of Jonathan Biggs finding a weak spot and ruthlessly exposing it. There was absolutely nothing more they could do.

He'd even tried to get the old Gradey cabin on the historical register, but the request was turned down, because the date of the building could not be substantiated. In the words of the secretary he spoke to in Washington, the Gradey cabin "wasn't historically significant." He had a feeling that Biggs had had a hand in that, too, but of course he had no proof. Proof. That's what it all boiled down to now. And proof was the one thing they didn't have.

There was no deed in existence for the Gradeys' land, no record of a bill of sale, no mention in the early surveying records of the county. Mr. Hamilton imagined the property had never even been surveyed. Back in 1800, Tom Rodgers had just claimed the land and walked it off to measure it. The Little Peavine Creek was one boundary, and local landmarks probably made up the others. Folks on adjoining claims did the same, and everybody respected one another's claims.

Then, in 1835, Tom sold the cabin to Jedediah Talmadge, who was Talley's ancestor, and either a formal deed was never made, or it was never filed with the proper authorities. He had heard of similar cases where things got straightened out all right, but it looked like this one was going to have an unhappy ending.

Elizabeth Gradey never spoke until they were back in Mr. Hamilton's office and Jonathan Biggs was gliding away in his sleek limo. Meg and Talley had begged to be allowed to wait in her father's office. They stood dejectedly by the window, staring out into the park, but not really seeing anything.

Mrs. Gradey's voice was unsteady. "I want you to know I appreciate everything you and your staff did to try to help us, Kenneth." She sank down wearily into a chair. "Nobody could have worked harder."

Mr. Hamilton put one arm around Meg and the other around Talley. "You know how I hate to give up on this thing, Elizabeth, but I'm afraid we're licked. Jonathan Biggs and Lebanon Hills Estates will forge ahead." He looked more tired than Meg had ever seen him look before.

"Talley and I are young and flexible, and I know we'll manage to get used to the apartment we found here in Lebanon, but I worry about Mim. I'm afraid losing her home will be the end of her." She searched in her purse for a tissue. "It's more than just a place to live for Mim. She was born there, and so was her father before her. She's a part of that house and the land . . . like a tree growing out of it. Oh, I can't really explain it, but I think you know what I mean. I know that Meg understands." Mrs. Gradey smiled at Meg, her eyes bright with tears.

"I think I understand, too," Kenneth Hamilton replied. "And I'm more sorry that things turned out this way than I could ever say."

Talley's mother blew her nose and managed a shaky laugh. "Well, I can't sit around here all day feeling sorry for myself." She stood up. "We've got a lot to do, don't we, son?"

Talley could only nod his head. Meg cleared her throat and said, "I told Talley that I'd be glad to help you with packing or cleaning or anything, Mrs. Gradey."

"Thank you, Meg. I will be glad to have the help."

"That goes for all of us, Elizabeth. Just call us when you're ready for some extra hands." Mr. Hamilton shook her hand, and then Talley's. "Hang in there, okay?" he said softly to Talley.

"I will, sir," Talley answered roughly. Then he quickly ran past his mother, head down, and out into the hall. He didn't want them to see him cry.

"Poor Talley," his mother sighed. "He'll have a hard time with this loss, too, I'm afraid. But my husband's death taught me that time really can help ease the pain of loss." She straightened her shoulders, as if she felt strengthened by remembering that.

"Well, Kenneth, I'll talk to you soon." Elizabeth Gradey smiled at Meg as she walked out the door. "Come over to see us soon, Meg. Mim will welcome the company, and so will Talley."

"That's a very brave lady there, Meg," Dad told her as Mrs. Gradey walked down the hall.

"She's a pioneer, now, too, isn't she, Dad?"

"She sure is, and Talley will be, too." Her father sighed and slowly rearranged the papers on his desk. "Let's head for home, Meggie girl. I could stand to see a bunch of happy, friendly faces after this afternoon."

"Even ones covered with graham crackers and dirt?"

"Those are the best kind." Dad turned off the light and shut the door.

* * *

Her father helped her move the cherry wood chest down the narrow attic stairs into her bedroom, and she spent the whole evening telling her parents and little brothers what she had learned about it and its contents.

Her mother was amazed. She went over the quilts and baby clothes carefully. "Look at the tiny stitches. Just think of the time it took to make these things!" she said over and over.

Even Micah and Daniel were impressed with the sampler that ten-year-old Sarah Randall had made. Micah was speechless for once when Meg retold Mim's story about Joshua Randall.

"Joshua Randall was really a Revolutionary War soldier, and this was his uniform jacket?" he whispered. "Meg, can I touch it?"

It made her feel good to know that her family felt the chest was as special as she did. Her father, though, voiced a thought that she had tried to keep to the back of her mind.

"When we bought this house, it was with all the contents included. But I feel that the remaining descendants of this Randall family should be notified of these things. After all, these are really family heirlooms, and they belong with those people." He ran his hand through his hair. "I know we bought it with the house, but we really don't have any right to it."

"But, Dad, those people don't deserve to have the Keepsake Chest!" Meg cried indignantly. "They sold it along with the house! They had forgotten all about it."

"Maybe they never knew it was there, Meg," her

mother said gently. "In the late 1920s the house was left to Rachel Rodgers's distant cousins. She had no close relations left. Those cousins lived somewhere out west, I remember the realtor said, and they were elderly themselves." Mrs. Hamilton frowned. "It seems like there would have to be some descendants of the Randalls around somewhere, but, really, Kenneth, how would we ever find them to let them know about the chest?"

"I don't know, Carin. I'll have to check into it, though." He turned to Meg. "You know we have to try to find the rightful owners, don't you, Punkin?"

"I know you're right, Dad. I just don't want to have to give the chest away to someone who won't really care about it, that's all."

Her mother gave her a hug. "Maybe we won't be able to trace them," she whispered in her ear.

Dad took the boys downstairs with the promise of chocolate ice-cream cones on the back porch, and Meg and her mother put the last quilt back in the chest.

"I wonder if the smell will ever come out of them?" Meg asked. "Do you think we could wash them?"

"I'd be afraid to do that. They might be too old. Maybe someone at a museum or even at the university in Columbus could tell us what to do." Her mother looked around Meg's room.

"You know, I still can't believe that this lovely wallpaper was put up so long ago. I must go over to visit Mim again. She's a remarkable woman." Mrs. Hamilton had gone over several times with Meg to the little cabin to see Elizabeth Gradey and Mim.

"I told Talley I'd be over when they start getting their

things packed up. Mrs. Gradey said she wanted to get it over with now that they knew they really had to leave." Meg felt her throat tighten and tears stung her eyes. "Oh, Mom, how could anyone be as mean as that horrible Jonathan Biggs?"

"I wish I knew the answer to that, Meg, but I don't. The only fortunate thing is that there are few people as totally awful as that man. And thank goodness for that."

"Talley's mother thinks that Mim will never be the same after they move. She won't die, will she?"

"Meg, you have to remember that Mim is a terribly old lady. She'll be ninety-six on her next birthday. She's lived a long life, longer than most people live, and she's been happy and healthy, too. People don't live forever, you know."

"I know, Mom, I know. But if Mim dies because she's been cheated out of her home, it'll mean that Jonathan Biggs is a murderer!" Meg didn't even try to keep the tears back now; she sobbed against her mother until she couldn't cry anymore.

"Meg, we're ready to go," Dad called up the stairs the next evening.

"I'll be right down." Meg finished brushing her hair, and straightened the bow on the front of her dress. Their whole family was going to the Gradey cabin for a party. Meg dreaded going, because it would be the last time she would see the place as it had always been. Mrs. Gradey had decided to start packing the next day.

Because they brought the little boys and Nicholas, they

drove down the road to the Gradeys'. The path along the Little Peavine would have been too treacherous in the dark. Twilight had deepened almost to night, and as they drove slowly down the lane, Mrs. Hamilton pointed to the cabin.

"Oh, look," she cried softly. "Elizabeth said this was going to be a special celebration, a joyful farewell to the place. Now I'm beginning to understand what she meant."

Meg leaned forward in her seat and looked out the front window past her mother. "Oh! Luminarias!" she gasped. "Look, Daniel and Micah!"

The porch and stone walk leading to the drive were lined with warmly glowing candlelit paper bags. It made the little house look as if it were set in the middle of a fairyland.

"Remember the year we spent the holidays in Santa Fe?" Mom asked. One year, before Nicholas had been born, they stayed with Mom's best friend from college and her family in New Mexico.

"I 'member," Daniel said solemnly.

"Oh, you do not," Micah told him. "*I* don't remember, and you're younger than me."

"Luminarias are a lovely tradition there on Christmas Eve," Mom explained, hoping to avoid an argument. "A little sand goes in the bottom of the bag, then a votive candle is set in the sand. The bags are spaced about two feet apart, along roads, sidewalks, and even on top of the flat-roofed adobe houses. Thousands of them are put out, just for that one special night, lining the narrow, twisting streets of New Mexican towns. They are put out to light the way of the Christ Child."

Inside the cabin's main room, candles provided the only light. Talley's mother was dressed in her costume from the Golden Lamb gift shop. Mim sat in her favorite place, looking small and frailer than ever, but still ramrod straight in her chair. Talley came in from the kitchen, carefully carrying a loaded tray.

"The luminarias are just beautiful, Elizabeth," Mrs. Hamilton said. Talley's mother smiled quietly.

"I know it's not the right season, but I'm hoping that if the Christ Child happened to be wandering around Ohio tonight, He'd see the lights and feel welcome here." She reached out and tousled Daniel's blond hair, trying to keep the mood light. "And if we ever needed Him, it's here tonight. A miracle would be a nice thing to have right about now."

"Oh, Elizabeth—" Meg's father started to say, but she stopped him.

"It's all right, Kenneth. I know that we've done all we could. I just can't seem to let go of a tiny flicker of hope. It's like those candles out there. No matter how often I tell myself that we've lost, I can't extinguish that little hope."

"That's right, Elizabeth. You keep that candle lit just as long as you can," a deep voice spoke from the door. Meg looked around to see Professor Greene smiling at them from the front porch.

"Come in here this minute, you dear man," Mim ordered from her rocking chair. The professor immediately obeyed. He seemed to fill the whole room with his huge form. Meg noticed that he carried a violin case with him.

"It's always a pleasure to see you, Hyrum," Mim told him as he stooped to kiss her cheek.

"Mim's the only person I've ever heard call the professor 'Hyrum,' " Talley whispered to Meg. "He's been friends of our family for years and years, but even my mom calls him 'Professor.' "

Meg had never seen the cabin in candlelight before, and it made her feel as if they had all magically slipped back into the past. Even though it was late June, a small fire burned in the huge stone fireplace.

"I had to have a little fire tonight," Talley's mother told them. "I know it's insane, but I couldn't bear to leave without having one last fire."

Soon Talley and Meg were busy helping Micah and Daniel shake a long-handled corn popper over the fire. The boys were thrilled, and decided it was just like camping out, only better. Nicholas had fallen asleep, and Dad gently laid him down on a quilt folded on the floor in the corner.

The grown-ups settled around Mim's chair. The tiny old lady looked at them without speaking for a moment. "Sometimes it feels to me that the past is alive all around us at times." She nodded her head. "Tonight is one of those times. I can almost see my grandfather, Jedediah, sitting before the fire there, and others, oh so many others."

"Ghosts, Mim?" Carin Hamilton asked.

"No, not ghosts. I just feel them here with us, their spirits are built into the very walls of this place. The past is not so far away as we think."

Kneeling by the fireplace, Meg felt a chill that traveled down her backbone, but ended in a warm, tingly feeling in her middle.

"I, too, have felt the past very near me at times." The professor nodded his great head in agreement. "Standing in the Valley of the Kings, in the Egyptian desert, and on the Mount of Olives in Jerusalem. I have felt it here, too."

"Do you believe in ghosts, Professor?" Talley asked, his blue eyes rounder than Meg had ever seen them before.

"If by the term ghosts you mean white sheets and chains at midnight, Talmadge, no, I do not." The professor smiled, and leaned back in his chair. "But I believe, as Mim does, that at special times, in special places, a thinning of the veil takes place."

"Veil?" Meg repeated.

"Yes, I believe that we are separated from those who have lived before us in this world by something as gossamer as a veil. It is over us, most of the time, separating us from the past. But there are times when the veil thins, and those with enough sensitivity and perception sense the thinning, and feel, and yes, sometimes even see things from that other realm."

Meg and Talley played go fish and Bohemian rummy with the boys at the kitchen table, but for the rest of the evening she thought about what the professor said. It was easy to let Micah and Daniel win with her mind so far away. She thought Talley was off with his own thoughts, too. The grown-ups sat in the living room, speaking quietly. Later the professor had promised to play a Vivaldi violin piece.

A thinning of the veil, the professor had called it. Was that what she had been feeling about the Keepsake Chest?

— *Thirteen* —

A WREN in the apple tree outside her window woke Meg up the next morning. When Talley had first showed her a wren, she had thought it was amazing that such a loud, lovely sound could come out of such a tiny, plain brown bird. And the name he called it! *Troglodytes*—something or other. What a name for a dainty thing like that!

She rolled over onto her stomach, smiling a little as she tried to repeat the Latin name. As she started to wake up more completely, she remembered the dream.

It all came flooding back to her, so vivid that at first she wondered if it could have been real. The wren outside continued to sing, and sunlight streamed through the airy Priscilla curtains.

It was hard to think that anything even remotely supernatural was possible in such an atmosphere; there was no fog rolling in over the brooding hills or owls hooting in dead trees, no graveyard, no clock striking twelve. And yet, the memory of the dream grew in her mind, until she sat up in her bed and had to pay attention to it.

She was in a small clearing in the dream. Huge trees crowded close, and scattered throughout the open space were large stumps, indicating that the land had only recently been cleared.

Two large white oxen were tethered close to where she stood, and she could hear them tearing up mouthfuls of the sparse grass. A blue jay dove across the clearing, startling her, but the oxen never flinched. Flies droned upward and then settled on their broad backs, and the oxen paid them no mind.

She was suddenly aware of the sound of an ax coming from the other side of the clearing, and walked toward that sound. The ringing of the ax grew louder, and she saw a man with a straw hat and a long brown beard working at a large tree. The ax bit through the rough brown bark and into the creamy wood of the tree.

After a while the man stopped to rest. He wiped his face with a handkerchief and took off his hat. That was when Meg noticed the wagon, and the lean-to tent made of canvas strung between two trees. A young boy was feeding twigs into a fire, and near him a woman crouched near a large flat tree stump, mixing something in a pot with a wooden spoon.

Meg walked toward the fire, and the woman looked up at her and smiled. Her face was thin, but strong, and her eyes were as green as Meg's own.

Then the woman spoke, but Meg could make no sense out of her words.

"Look in the chest, girl, in the cherry wood chest, and all will be well. The rightful owners will get their due in the end," she said. She talked to Meg as if she knew her, and after she spoke, she continued to mix the cornmeal in the iron pot.

Meg walked on past the woman and the little boy, and stood at the entrance of the shelter. Inside were the things that must have once ridden in the wagon—barrels and boxes of food, a plow blade and some pieces of farm equipment, blankets and clothing neatly stacked—and the Keepsake Chest. Its color was lighter, but Meg recognized the vine heart and the initials of Joshua Randall and his bride. And suddenly Meg knew where she was, and who the woman and the man were.

Her dream had taken her to the spot where Talley's cabin stood, and she watched as Tom Rodgers cut the first logs for the house. She saw the temporary shelter Tom had made from the canvas that had covered his wagon. She saw Tom's wife Sarah fixing supper, and his little boy building the fire to cook it; Sarah, as a young woman, not the wrinkled, dignified old lady in Mim's portrait.

Meg got out of bed and knelt at her window. The early morning air touched her face gently, fresh and clean. She wrinkled her forehead as she tried to remember the words Sarah Rodgers said to her.

" 'Look in the chest. The cherry wood chest.' " She whispered the words out loud, and they seemed to echo around her room. " 'The rightful owners will get their due'? What does that mean?"

She had never thought much about dreams, but then she had never had one that seemed so real. What could it mean? "Look in the chest." She had already looked in the chest, and knew what she had found.

She stared out the window without seeing the tree

or the fields beyond. Could there be anything else?

She got up and walked over to the chest. "This is ridiculous," she tried to tell herself. "I don't even know what I'm looking for." Open the chest, something told her, even stronger.

The quilts were lying on top. One by one she took each one out, and carefully worked her fingers over the entire surface. Was there something hidden in the filling? Paper would crinkle if she touched it, and gold coins or silver would feel lumpy. In spite of her common sense, she began to get excited. Was there something valuable hidden in the chest after all?

It took her a long time to check every square inch of the quilts, and her hands ached when she was through. She found nothing.

The baby clothes and the blue shawl were too light and delicate to hide anything, and she laid them on her bed. She held the sampler made by Sarah Randall in the sunlight at the window. She looked closely at the embroidery. Maybe there was a clue there.

Meg sighed and straightened her back. Her shoulders hurt from hunching over the work. She looked again at the neat letters and numbers, the childishly designed but beautifully sewn house and animals. Could there be anything hidden in the design? After several minutes she put the sampler, too, on her bed, and picked up the blue army coat that Joshua Randall had worn.

She'd never been very interested by history, but since they moved to Ohio, she had been surrounded by it. Before, history had seemed like something remote, something hardly real; now it was as alive as her dream had been. Now she held a piece of history right in her hands.

With the greatest of care, she felt the sleeves, the front, and the back of the wool jacket. She turned the collar up, and ran her hands inside the coat as well. Nothing. There was nothing hidden in the jacket, or in anything else in the chest.

She put everything away. What a dumb thing to do, all because of a dream. She shook her head and grinned at her own foolishness. But almost immediately another voice seemed to speak in her head. The words were the words Sarah Rodgers said to her in her dream.

"Look in the chest, girl, the cherry wood chest, and all will be well. The rightful owners will get their due in the end."

Meg shrugged her shoulders with impatience. She couldn't figure it out. She didn't see how it could be important.

She couldn't understand it, but she had a good idea who could. Hurriedly she pulled on a pair of shorts and a shirt and stuck her feet into a pair of sneakers. She ran downstairs, and after a quick word with her mother in the kitchen, ran out the back door, down around the barn, and through the woods to the log-and-stone house.

It was before eight o'clock, but already Talley and his mother were emptying closets.

"We have a system all worked out," Talley told her. "One pile is for things we want to save, another pile is for things to go to the Salvation Army thrift store, and the third pile is for junk to just throw out." Meg looked at Talley's three piles. The largest one was of things to save.

Talley gave a little laugh that had no joy in it. "I know, I know. It's hard to throw anything out. Some of this stuff has probably been around here for a hundred years." He scrambled in the pile of stuff from the closet. "Look at these. Aren't they great?" He held up a pair of black high-top shoes that buttoned up the sides. "Mim said that these were hers when she was a girl. Can you imagine how long it would take to get dressed in the morning when you had to button up these?"

Meg shook her head. "Your house is like a museum, you know that?" Talley stopped smiling. It wouldn't be his house much longer. It wouldn't be anyone's house.

Quickly Meg continued. "I need to talk to you about a dream I had last night. Can you come outside for a minute?"

"Sure," Talley said, and he led the way out to the lawn around the cabin.

Meg took the time now to look around her. She had seen this very piece of ground as it looked in the year 1800 in her dream. It was all so strange, and yet in a way it seemed perfectly normal, perfectly right. As she and Talley walked through the still-wet grass, she told him about seeing Tom and Sarah Rodgers, newly arrived from New Jersey and just starting to build their log cabin.

"And I can't help feeling that what Sarah Rodgers said to me in the clearing is really important. I can't explain how or why. And I can't help feeling that somehow you are involved in it, too." She stopped and gave him a long look. "Do you think I'm totally crazy?"

"No, of course not! I'm just trying to figure out what Sarah meant. What will we find in the chest that can make everything all right?" Talley stopped walking and pulled a tall piece of grass out of the ground. Absently he began to chew it. "It's just like what the professor said, isn't it? The thinning of the veil between us and the past." Suddenly he dropped the grass and turned to her, excited.

"Meg, do you think that it could be something to do with saving this land from Jonathan Biggs and his fancy houses?"

" 'The rightful owners will get their due in the end.' That was what she said!" Meg began to feel like they were on to something. "I think that anybody who loved this place would be upset at what Jonathan Biggs is trying to do. Sarah and Tom built this cabin and cleared the land, and they must have loved it very much. If there are ghosts or spirits or people from the past watching over this place, maybe they're trying to help us save it." She stopped, embarrassed. "What do you think, Talley?"

"I don't know if I believe in ghosts, but you may be right. I've heard Mim say that Miss Rachel's grandmother loved her new house, the one you're living in, but she always had a special love for her little log cabin." He was quiet for a long while, then he sighed. "But now what? What do we do now? It sounds like you've searched everything in the chest."

Meg's excitement drained away. "I wish I knew what to do next. I have a feeling that we're close to something—"

Her next words died away as the rumble of a whole string of large trucks reached them down the long gravel drive from the road. One of the trucks had a bulldozer on a trailer behind it.

Meg's mouth fell open. "What's going on?" she cried. "How can they be starting already?"

Talley's face had gotten very white. "My mother got a phone call last night from Jonathan Biggs's lawyer. Somehow they got special permission from the county to start clearing the land now, even before we move." He jerked his eyes away from the trucks and workmen who were now setting up surveying equipment and driving red-flagged stakes into the ground. "At least they can't tear down the house until we're gone," he said bitterly. "But that's why Mom decided to pack and leave as soon as possible and not wait the thirty days. She said she couldn't bear to see the destruction of the land and trees." Talley sniffed. "Or of her garden," he finished in almost a whisper, and then angrily wiped away the tears Meg pretended not to see.

"Talley, we've got to do something, and it has to be right away. We don't have much time left." She didn't know what to do, but the thought immediately came into her mind as though someone had whispered it.

"Come with me, quick!" She grabbed Talley by the arm and ran toward home.

—*Fourteen*—

THEY were halfway across the sunny clearing before Talley was able to gasp out a few words.

"Would . . . you . . . explain?" was all he could manage. They were running flat out now, Meg first, over the path by Little Peavine Creek. Talley was trying to keep his glasses up on his nose with one hand while Meg dragged him by the other.

"Can't yet . . . want to make sure . . ." Her breath came in jagged gasps. "Just hurry!"

Their tennis shoes pounded on the hard-packed dirt of the sun-dappled path. In the distance they could hear Jonathan Biggs's workmen shouting to each other, and as they passed under the Big Oak, the massive rumble of a bulldozer being started ripped through them like a rifle shot. They ran even faster.

It was quiet in the attic. The destruction about to take place not far away could not enter here. The early morning light made the center of the room appear rosy, but the edges of the attic, where the ceiling followed the pitch of the roof, were dark.

The children stood at the top of the stairs, gasping for breath. As soon as she could speak, Meg said, "I should have thought about looking at the papers a long time ago."

"Papers? There were old papers in the chest?"

"The whole packet must have slipped off the blanket, and I never gave it another thought." She moved to the place where the chest had been. "It's got to be right around here."

Talley dropped to his knees and looked under a battered white metal cabinet. He straightened up and began to move some cardboard boxes. Nothing was behind them.

Meg was thinking. "That first time I opened the chest, I put the blanket down right about here." She gestured with her arms.

Talley ducked his head as he followed the sloping ceiling to the wall. He almost disappeared in the shadows, but immediately called out, "I found it! It was almost against the wall."

Together they sat on the dusty floor. "I thought they were just boring old letters or something." Meg's fingers shook as she picked at the string holding the papers together. She carefully laid each piece of paper out on the floor.

There appeared to be many letters, the ink faded to tan on paper spotted with age. Meg opened up a folded document. It was hard to make out the writing, and the spelling and punctuation was funny, but she haltingly read aloud.

*On this the Twentie-ninth day of Oct., in the
yere of our Lord One thousend seventeen and
seventy fore, was sealed together in marrage befor
me Josh. Randall and Callie Parker.*
*The reverennd Thom. Avery
circut Minister*

*Hopewell, inn the Colony of
new Jersey*

She looked up. "Callie Parker. Now we know who
Joshua made this chest for." Her heart had stopped pound-
ing now; she was calm and sure of everything. She gently
refolded the marriage certificate and put it on top of the
letters.

The last bit of paper in the packet was small, but
immediately, before she even read it, she knew it was the
proof that the Gradeys needed to save their home.

She could almost feel them all in the room—Joshua,
who had built the chest, and Callie, his wife. She seemed
to see again the dark hair and bright green eyes of Sarah
at the cabin clearing, and the strong, thick figure of her
husband, Tom Rodgers, with his ax. She felt the presence
of Sarah's granddaughter, Miss Rachel. It was a feeling that
afterward she would find impossible to describe; not at all
frightening, like in a ghost story or a scary movie on late
at night. She felt close to all those people—she actually
felt they were near, and watching, and very, very happy.

"This is it, Talley." She spoke softly, so as not to
disturb the deep peace that was present in the room. Talley

looked at her with shining eyes, and she knew he felt it, too.

She unfolded the thin, brown paper. The ink with which it had been written was still dark, and the writing was clear. There were few words; it took only a moment to read it aloud.

Rec'd of Jedediah Talmadge this day 125 dollars in cash money as payment for twenty-five acres of land and a log house on the Little Peavine, Bordered by said Creek on the West to the marked red oak, South to Cooper's Ridge, east to the Peabody Farm, and due north to Asa Matlock's claim.

Thom. Rodgers
12th day of May, 1835
Warren County in the state
of Ohio

The next hour would always be a confused whirl in Meg's mind. She remembered rushing downstairs, with Talley right behind her, and the both of them trying to explain to her mother what they had found. It didn't take Mrs. Hamilton too long to understand that something important had indeed been found, and before Talley and Meg were around the corner of the house, she had Mr. Hamilton on the phone.

The children flew over the ground back to the Gradeys' log cabin. Later, the foreman for Jonathan Biggs's earthmoving crew said he would never forget how suddenly, from out of nowhere, a skinny little girl appeared right in front of his machine and refused to move.

"There she stood," he told his buddies at the Town Café that day after work. "She had her arms across her chest, and kept shouting something. 'Course, I couldn't hear her till I turned off my 'dozer. Then she came across loud and clear! 'Stop until my lawyer gets here!' is what she kept yellin'. So I stopped. There was no way I could get her to move, that's what. I figured she was another one of those crazy environmentalist types, although she was kind of young. And the kid with her was even younger. Reddest hair you'd ever hope to see. None of us minded taking a break, anyway. It wasn't long before the little girl's lawyer did show up." He took a long drink of his iced tea, set it down again, and chuckled. "But the fireworks didn't really start till Biggs showed up. I've never seen the ol' boy so red in the face! And yelling and screaming to beat the band!"

None of his men could really say that they liked Jonathan Biggs, and the guys at the table all laughed at the thought of their cool, businesslike boss so upset.

"I have to hand it to the little girl's lawyer. He didn't budge an inch. Stood right up to Biggs, calm and quiet as you please. Before too long, a regular crowd of people had gathered. Biggs's lawyer and secretary came, and they were as mad as Biggs was himself. A woman and three little boys, and another woman with a tiny old lady on her arm stayed on the porch of the cabin. They all looked pretty happy about an old piece of paper the little girl had found."

The foreman rubbed a grimy hand over the stubble on his chin. "I was glad when the boss finally yelled at us to go on ahead to the next job. That old log cabin was in a real pretty spot, and I sure hated to have to tear it down, and clear out all those big trees. It would have been a darn shame, that's what." He drank again, and shook his head. "Those people were all mighty happy, laughin' and cryin' and huggin' each other. Never saw anything like it, that's what."

— *Fifteen* —

MEG leaned her head wearily against the backseat and closed her eyes. Going to the mall in Cincinnati had been fun, but tiring. She'd be glad to get back to the peace and quiet of the farm. She smiled at the change in herself.

Nicholas was fast asleep in his car seat, and next to her Micah and Daniel slumped against each other like two sleep-fjing puppies. In the front seat her parents talked quietly about the wicker porch furniture they had picked out that day.

"They'll be delivering it on Thursday, Kenneth. What do you say to having a party Friday night? We'll have Elizabeth and Mim and Talley, and maybe the professor."

"I think that's a great idea. We all have a lot to celebrate, don't we?"

"We have a lot to be thankful for. I really think it would have been the end of Mim if they had lost the cabin."

The steady drone of the engine and the soft murmur of her parents' voices was hypnotizing. The last thought she had was that a party would be fun to plan.

Meg stood at the sink, mixing more lemonade, when she heard Micah's friends outside.

"Micah's sister almost got run over by a bulldozer. My dad said."

"Naw, she didn't. My mom heard all about it at the grocery store in Lebanon. She knocked all the surveyor's stakes out of the ground as soon as they stuck 'em in."

Meg leaned over the sink to look out the window. Micah sat on the railing of the back porch, kicking his feet rhythmically against the spindles.

She knew what he was waiting for. Pretty soon one of the boys he played ball with would say, "Hey Micah, what was it that real estate man said?" and he'd be off again, making them roll on the ground with laughter. He could make his face turn as red as Jonathan Biggs's face had been, that morning at the Gradey cabin. He had done this same performance many times during the past week.

Meg stifled a groan. "I wish he'd just keep quiet about it all," she thought. "I wish everyone would just forget the whole thing. Everything's going to be all right now. It's embarrassing to have people talk about it all the time." She put the wooden spoon in the sink and set the pitcher on the tray with a plate of brownies.

As she walked past the refrigerator, she looked at the newspaper article Mom had stuck there with magnets. "It isn't every day that our daughter gets her picture in the paper," she told Meg.

"Or that she is able to save our neighbors' home and defeat the richest, toughest businessman in Ohio with a combination of brains and bravery," Dad had chimed in.

"Cut it out, you two!" Meg pretended to be mad, but she had to smile all the same. She knew they were proud of what she had done, and she figured that she could handle a little teasing about it.

They had spent the whole day getting ready for the party. The new wicker furniture looked great on the front porch. It was fun to see the big dining room filled with people, too. It was the first time they had used it. Mom had baked French bread, and made her famous chicken and shrimp and rice dish from Spain, and Dad tossed the green salad with his own secret dressing. Meg had made the brownies first thing in the morning, before it got too hot.

She carried the tray out onto the porch. The mist was beginning to rise in the fields across the road, and soon fireflies would punctuate the shadows with their special light.

Mim was speaking, and her soft, gravelly voice reminded Meg of the sounds an old house makes—the creaks and rumblings of the old wood, the settling of it all into its foundations.

"I can't say when I've enjoyed anything more, dear," she said to Mrs. Hamilton. "It is wonderful to see Miss Rachel's house lived in again, and loved, too. There's just something ever so sad about a house all dark and empty. Many a time I have looked through the woods, and remembered how the windows of this house would shine with lamplight, but see nothing but dark."

Mim leaned back against the padded cushion, all dressed up in her best black, with a lacy white collar set off by her gold oval pin. A faraway look was in her dark eyes. Meg imagined again that the old lady was seeing things long since gone. Mim's white knitted shawl was folded over her knees in spite of the warmth of the summer evening. She looked very tiny and thin, as though the slightest breeze would blow her away from them.

Meg felt her heart jump with happiness, as it had every time she'd seen Mim since that day when they knew the log house legally belonged to the Gradeys. The old lady's eyes had lost the dead, dull look that Meg had noticed in them during that awful time when they thought they had lost their home. She was so glad she had been able to help Mim and Talley, and Mrs. Gradey. She was so glad that they had found the bill of sale in time.

She didn't even mind that now she'd lose the Keepsake Chest. Dad had been looking for the descendants of Joshua and Callie Randall; even Professor Greene had joined in the search, and it would only be a matter of time before the rightful owners were found. She stifled a sigh. "I only hope that whoever gets it will appreciate what they have, and not let it sit forgotten in a basement or an attic somewhere," she said to herself over and over again.

"Ah, here's more of that marvelous lemonade." Professor Greene's basso profundo voice filled the porch. Meg put the tray down on the low, round table.

"May I pour you another glass, Professor?" Mrs. Hamilton asked.

"Thank you so much." The professor smiled at her and held out his glass. "You know," he continued, "Meg would be interested in what we have been talking about, since she has such an interest in the history of this area." He looked at her and let his black eyes twinkle, to let her know he couldn't resist teasing her about the day she went to him for help and hadn't been completely honest. She hadn't really been interested in the history of the whole area, more like the history of one particular family.

"She would be, I'm sure," Talley spoke up from his place on the top porch step.

Not so very long ago, she wouldn't have cared two cents for history of any sort, especially of the town of Lebanon, in Warren County, Ohio. But she knew now that she cared very much about it, that somehow it was a part of her. It was more than finding the Keepsake Chest and the proof needed to save Talley's home, although that was certainly part of it. The whole thing went much deeper than that, in some way that she didn't yet understand.

She suddenly realized that Professor Greene was speaking again. "We have just been talking of what I like to call the abolition era in Warren County. This countryside was a route of the Underground Railroad, and in fact, that accounts for my interest in and my retirement to this place." He looked around the group seated on the porch. "One of my own ancestors was a runaway slave, and came safely through here to Canada. Stories I remembered hearing about him in my family first interested me in the houses along the Little Peavine. That small water course out there"—he motioned with his hand toward the meadow beyond the barn—"was a major route of the Railroad."

For a second everyone spoke at once. Meg was thrilled at this further tie to the past. She thought of the people who must have traveled over this ground, frightened, weary, hunted like animals, but desperate to escape the bondage they had been subjected to.

She watched the professor closely, and saw that he

had more to say, and was waiting for the general hubbub of conversation to cease. He had an actor's voice and an actor's sense of timing, too. She could tell he had something else to say to them, something important.

As everyone became quiet again, he held up his hand for their attention. "In fact," he rumbled, "one of the letters Meg found in Joshua Randall's chest proves a theory I've spent years formulating." He really had their attention now. "One of the letters you kindly let me examine was from Levi Coffin, who was known as the leader of the Underground Railroad, and who helped thousands of slaves escape. The letter was written to Sarah Randall Rodgers."

He paused and sipped his lemonade, his soft black, wise eyes wandering over them all. "I've always believed that this house, and that the Gradeys' log cabin, were important stations on the Underground Railroad, and that Sarah Randall Rodgers and Jedediah Talmadge were conductors, who helped escaped slaves hide and then move along to the next station. The letter proves that my assumptions have been correct."

"This is what we need to have your cabin placed on the National Register, Elizabeth," Dad exclaimed to Talley's mother. "They'll be begging you to list it!"

"And no one will ever be able to bulldoze it down!" Talley said.

Now there was a real hubbub on the front porch. Everyone was excited by the professor's announcement, and everyone talked at once. Micah and Daniel, just back from running through the yard, demanded to know what they had missed. Callahan barked until Dad quieted him.

"It's incredible!" Talley's mother said. "I never heard

any family stories about the Underground Railroad that I can remember. Did you, Mim?"

"Nobody talked much about it," the old woman answered. "But I do know there were rumors. 'Course, it was all very secret. That was the most important thing."

"That's true," Professor Greene agreed. "In fact, we know very little about how the Railroad worked, because of the absolute secrecy that enveloped it. After all, it was a federal offense to aid in the escape of slaves, and some of the people who were caught working the Railroad were imprisoned. Sadly, most of its story died with the people it saved."

Meg's father finally quieted everyone down. "That's not all the news for tonight," he told them. Professor Greene leaned back in his chair, with a big smile on his face, and Meg saw that whatever it was her father was about to tell them, the professor was in on it.

Her father stood up and cleared his throat. "As all of you know, I've been doing some checking the last week or so about the family that built this house, the same family who before that built the Gradeys' cabin.

"We felt that the chest Meg discovered in the attic of this house did not rightfully belong to us, despite the fact that we purchased the place with its contents included in the sale." He walked a few steps up and down the porch, almost as if he were in a courtroom, and Meg squirmed impatiently. She hated the thought of losing the chest. If he had found out who it belonged to, she wished he'd make the announcement and get it over with.

"I must admit that certain names had interested me even before Meg found the chest, and after she and Talley started doing research, I began a little research of my own.

"Let me tell you a story," he continued—"a brief story," he said with a smile in Meg's direction as he heard her impatient sigh. "It's a little complicated, but I've tried to simplify it, so it won't take long, I promise.

"Meg, you and the boys probably remember that our family has its roots in Ohio."

"Well, yes. That's one of the reasons you wanted to move here." Meg couldn't figure out what this had to do with anything. "You always said that for some reason you felt like Ohio was home." Meg never understood it before; now she felt exactly the same way.

"I did a little checking with my mother in Florida, and she helped start me in the right direction. And Professor Greene and Mrs. Gradey proved to be of great help in the genealogical end of things."

Meg noticed now that Mrs. Gradey was smiling, too. Meg shook her head in confusion. Did everybody know what was going on but her?

"Well, I said I would be brief, and I will." Dad stopped walking now right in front of her. "The cousins Miss Rachel Rodgers left this house to lived in California, and their name was Wilson. A pretty common name, and at the time I remember thinking briefly that my grandmother's maiden name had been Wilson. Just sort of a passing thought."

"Dad, wait a minute," Meg pleaded. She needed a moment to think. A chill ran over her in spite of the warmth of the night. What was her father saying? Could all this possibly be leading to where she now began to think it might? Could it be anything more than coincidence that brought them to this house in Ohio?

That brought her to the Keepsake Chest?

That brought her the vivid image of Sarah, a young Sarah with eyes as green as her very own?

"Do you mean we're related to them, Dad? To Sarah and Tom? And to Joshua Randall and Callie Parker? And Miss Rachel, too?" Was that shaky voice really hers?

Her father shook his head. "That's what I was hoping to be able to tell you. I had the whole Genealogy Club at the historical society working to try to tie us into the family. But we couldn't do it. There's a chance we are, but we just can't prove it yet. Some of the old records we need just aren't in existence anymore.

"The really interesting thing is the conversation I had with the people we bought this house from. The house had been left to them by Miss Rachel's cousins. They weren't related to them, and that means they really have no claim on the chest."

"I think that you are the one who was meant to have the chest, Meg," her mother said softly.

Talley's face split into an enormous grin, and Mim's wrinkled brown button of a face echoed it.

"I felt something all along was right, and special, some-how, about you, Meg Hamilton, you and your family." Mim's gentle voice whispered but reached them all clearly. "It doesn't matter whether or not you can prove you are really related to Joshua Randall and his descendants. You Hamiltons all belong here. You were sent here special to us, to save a place that was the heart of our family."

"Of both our families," Talley said. He pushed his funny round glasses up on his nose and grinned at her. "Welcome home, Meg."

With tears in her eyes, Meg thought about what the professor had said. It seemed to her that this was a time when the veil was very thin. She looked around her at the people she loved best in the world, some she had loved all her life, and the others she had only recently learned to love. They made a circle, all of them, there on the front porch.

But the circle didn't stop with her family and friends. It radiated out to those who had lived in this place before them: to Miss Rachel, and her love of life; to Tom and Sarah Rodgers, who came through the wilderness to build their lives; to Joshua and Callie, and the family they started in a new country they helped create.

Meg felt them all around her, felt their love. Mim was right. Her father might never be able to prove that Joshua and Callie, and Tom and Sarah were a part of their family. But Meg knew that it had to be true.

Life is changing and adjusting and growing all the time, Dad told her. Moving to Ohio had given her lots of opportunities to adjust . . . and to grow.

When she met Talley, she didn't even want to get to know him. Now he was her best friend.

Mim's great age had frightened her at first. But now when she looked at Mim, Meg saw a wise and warm human being, a wonderful bit of living history.

She had come to this place hating it. She thought she was a stranger, out of place and alone. Now, in the warm circle of these dear people, past and present, she saw where she really was. Home.